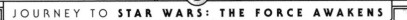

MOVING TARGET

A PRINCESS LEIA ADVENTURE

WRITTEN BY
CECIL CASTELLUCCI
AND
JASON FRY

ILLUSTRATED BY
PHIL NOTO

DISNEP
LUCASFILM
PRESS

LOS ANGELES • NEW YORK

For information address Disney · Lucasfilm Press,
1101 Flower Street, Glendale, California 91201.

Printed in the United States of America

First Edition, September 2015

3 5 7 9 10 8 6 4 2

FAC-020093-15278

ISBN 978-1-4847-2497-2

Library of Congress Control Number on file

Reinforced binding

Designed by Jason Wojtowicz

Visit the official *Star Wars* website at: www.starwars.com.

SUSTAINABLE FORESTRY INITIATIVE   Certified Sourcing
www.sfiprogram.org
SFI-00993

THIS LABEL APPLIES TO TEXT STOCK

PART THREE

A long time ago in a galaxy far, far away. . . .

Reeling from their disastrous defeat on Hoth, the heroic freedom fighters of the REBEL ALLIANCE have scattered throughout space, pursued by the agents of the sinister GALACTIC EMPIRE.

One rebel task force protects PRINCESS LEIA, bearing her in secrecy from star to star. As the last survivor of Alderaan's House of Organa, Leia is a symbol of freedom, hunted by the Empire she has opposed for so long.

The struggle against Imperial tyranny has claimed many rebel lives. As the Empire closes in, Leia resolves to make a sacrifice of her own, lest the cause of freedom be extinguished from the galaxy. . . .

PROLOGUE

PZ-4CO WAS BACK, and this time Leia Organa was too weary to come up with a good excuse that would send her away.

"General Organa, I have been requested to assist you in recording your memoirs," the tall, blue-plated protocol droid said. "I have made seven previous requests. When I made my first request forty-four days ago, you said—"

"I remember what I said, Peazy," Leia interrupted, leaning against the doorway that led into her quarters. The droid looked at her uncertainly, clearly having expected to be invited inside.

"When I made the second request thirty-eight days ago, your stated reason—"

"We're not going over all seven requests and how I responded to them," Leia said, folding her arms.

Suddenly, C-3PO's many odd habits didn't seem so bad. "Now remind me again why this is so important?"

The droid cocked her head at Leia, who allowed herself a slight smile. Peazy's programming hadn't anticipated that question.

"I would imagine the reason is obvious," PZ-4CO said. "You were a critically important member of the Rebel Alliance during the Galactic Civil War, a veteran of key battles such as Yavin, Hoth, and Endor—"

"That was a long time ago," Leia said, her eyes turning cold. "We're on the brink of war again—one we may not survive. In which case none of those things will matter."

"Those things are essential," the droid objected. "You are the leader of the Resistance, a critical check on the designs of the First Order. You are a symbol of the Resistance and an inspiration to all soldiers who follow our cause and do their duty in hard times."

"Duty," Leia said, smiling sadly, then shook her head.

"I have given offense somehow," the droid said tentatively.

"You haven't. But those are someone else's words. Who have you been talking to, Peazy?"

"Major Ematt has been very helpful in preparing me to interview you," the droid said.

"I might have known," Leia said, smiling at the

mention of the man she had fought alongside for so many years.

"Very well, I surrender," she said, indicating that the droid should come inside. "Where would you like to begin? No, never mind. You mentioned duty. As it happens, I've been thinking about that, too—about a lesson I learned many years ago. It's one I think every member of the Resistance would do well to master."

PART
ONE

CHAPTER 01

IMPERIAL ATTACK

BY THE TIME they saw the TIE fighters, it was too late.

Princess Leia Organa didn't even know the name of the system they were flying through—it was little more than a small dim sun, a pale purple gas giant, and a vast field of rocks and dust that gravity hadn't quite managed to squeeze into a planet.

Sensor operators aboard Leia's Nebulon-B frigate, the *Remembrance*, had spotted the Imperial fighters winging through the tumbling rocks—which meant the TIEs had also spotted the rebels. They wheeled out of the asteroids and bore down on the small rebel convoy: the *Remembrance*, two GR-75 transports, and a quartet of blockade runners.

As klaxons began to hoot aboard the *Remembrance*, Leia crossed the bridge to stand beside Captain Volk

Aymeric. The green-skinned Ishi Tib stared up at a holographic representation of the system, the locations of the rebel and Imperial ships marked by arrows and crosses. Aymeric held his arms calmly behind his back, but his eyestalks were quivering faintly.

Leia forced herself to say nothing. She was one of the principal leaders of the Rebellion, but Aymeric commanded the ship. It made for an awkward relationship. Leia didn't want Aymeric's crew to think she was telling their captain what to do, and she knew the Ishi Tib officer felt the same way about having an important rebel leader aboard his ship. They were always saying too much to each other, or too little.

"Send our starfighter pickets to intercept—and step up your scans," Aymeric ordered.

"Those are short-range fighters," Leia said. "And there are no known bases in this system. That's why we took this course through hyperspace."

Aymeric's left eyestalk swiveled in her direction, and he opened his beak in what she'd learned was his species' version of a frown.

"Exactly," he said. "Which means there's a carrier out there. Patch the audio from the fighters into—"

"Captain!" yelled a sensor officer. "Three ships coming out of hyperspace in sector three-F!"

"Pull the fighters back to defend the convoy," Aymeric said.

The bridge was a flurry of activity. Sensors painted the new arrivals as a trio of *Arquitens*-class light cruisers—an identification quickly confirmed by a bridge officer. Leia could picture them hurtling through space—elongated triangles with forked snouts, attached to three cylindrical engines.

Someone fed the transmissions sent by the six X-wing pilots on patrol into the bridge comm system, filling the space around them with chatter. Aymeric's eyestalks pivoted independently to look at the holographic display and focus on members of the bridge crew calling out new information.

"The cruisers are scrambling fighters!" a crew member warned.

"Fire at will," Aymeric said. "Order all craft to calculate the jump into hyperspace—we'll regroup at the rendezvous point determined by scatter protocol Besh."

The *Remembrance*'s turbolasers began to fire, and the deck beneath their feet shook slightly with each blast of energy sent out into space.

At Aymeric's side, Leia clenched her hands into fists. She was useless there. She felt like she was standing alongside her adoptive parents, Bail and Breha, waiting through one of Alderaan's endless royal ceremonies and knowing that she could let no emotion show on her face—because it would be seen and talked about. She'd once complained to one of her aunts that being a princess had to be about more than silently doing one's duty—only to have her aunt reply, with a sad smile, that she'd just described most of a princess's job.

"Are there any other rebel units within hailing range?" Leia asked, hating the idea of being chased off by three of the Empire's smaller warships.

"Negative," Aymeric said. "With the Empire looking for us everywhere, the fleet is completely scattered—broken into small convoys like ours. It's safer that way."

Except when we need help and there's none to be had, Leia thought.

She saw flashes of light through the broad viewports of the *Remembrance*'s bridge and felt the frigate shudder as laser fire splashed across its shields.

They heard an X-wing pilot howl, his voice rising and then vanishing in static. One of the crosses on Aymeric's holographic display blinked and vanished. Another rebel had lost his life, meaning another grim message sent to fall like a lightning strike on the heart of a parent or sweetheart. How many was that now? She shied away from even attempting such a terrible calculation.

Three of the blockade runners jumped into the safety of hyperspace. The X-wings were streaking for safety, as well. Leia could hear their pilots urging their astromech droids to make the navigational calculations more quickly.

"Captain, I have a priority signal from the *Ranolfo*," a young lieutenant called, identifying one of the blockade runners. "They've lost their starboard shields."

"How long till they can make the jump into hyperspace?" Aymeric asked.

The lieutenant spoke urgently into his headset, then shook his head. "At least three minutes."

"Captain, our course is locked in and we're ready to jump," the helmsman called.

"We're leaving them?" Leia asked.

Heads turned on the bridge and Aymeric's beak opened. "Turn to oh-thirty-eight to cover them," he said, not looking at Leia.

The *Remembrance* banked to starboard, turbolasers spitting fire in an effort to keep the swarming TIEs away from the vulnerable blockade runner. Leia stared grimly at the display hanging in the air in front of her—three crosses and far too many arrowheads.

Then the *Remembrance* lurched and a shudder rolled through it, followed by a groan and the wail of alarms.

"Damage report!" Aymeric barked.

"Hull breach just forward of the connecting spar— and secondary shields are down to fifteen percent!"

The Ishi Tib's shoulders slumped. "Make the jump to hyperspace on my command."

"Captain—" Leia began, but Aymeric turned to her, his voice quiet so only she could hear.

"I won't let the men and women aboard the *Ranolfo* die in vain, Princess," he said. "They have the same mission as every being in this convoy—and that's to keep you safe."

Leia looked away, forcing herself to unclench her fists, to breathe. Her face was impassive when she looked back at Aymeric and nodded. She barely registered the sound of the command he barked at the navigator or the sight of the stars elongating into streaks as the *Remembrance* vanished into hyperspace, leaving the doomed blockade runner behind.

CHAPTER 02

THE COST OF DUTY

WHEN LEIA LEFT the *Remembrance*'s bridge, a familiar figure was waiting on the other side of the door—a protocol droid with golden plating.

C-3PO started to say something, but she kept walking, forcing him to hurry along beside her, his servomotors whining. She'd ordered him to stay off the bridge—their situation was stressful enough without Threepio's incessant fretting and complaining.

The droid belonged to Luke Skywalker but had been lent to Leia to assist with etiquette and protocol when she met with secret delegations from planets that could aid the Rebellion in its war to overthrow the Empire. As the former senator from Alderaan, Leia was at ease in such meetings, able to call on a lifetime of diplomatic training.

But there had been no such meetings recently—just endless flight through space in an effort to stay one step ahead of Imperial patrols. After the Alliance's disastrous defeat on the ice planet Hoth, Mon Mothma and the rebel leadership had ordered the fleet to break into small task forces that were constantly jumping from star system to star system.

Mothma had explained that the safeguards were designed to prevent another defeat for Imperial propagandists to celebrate. But Leia worried that the constant flight made the Alliance look weak when it needed to convince people that the Emperor's grip could be broken. The Alliance had to gather its forces again—and win victories on the battlefield.

"Mistress Leia, where are you going?" C-3PO asked plaintively, shuffling along in her wake as quickly as he could.

"To my quarters," Leia said without turning. "I assume you remember where they are?"

"Of course I do," said Threepio, whose knowledge of etiquette somehow didn't include recognizing sarcasm. "My memory banks contain schematics of every ship to which I've been assigned while serving the Alliance."

"That's an excellent use of your memory banks, considering how many of those ships are now space dust."

Rebels saluted Leia as she passed. She wanted to cringe each time someone did that but forced herself to nod in return. It was a sign of respect for her as their superior, but they were not her friends.

She had never had many friends. She'd been too focused on the mission for which Bail Organa had trained her practically since birth—the overthrow of the Empire that had destroyed so much. But then Luke entered her life—along with Han Solo and Chewbacca.

Threepio said something that didn't register, because she was thinking of the last time she'd seen Han—of his eyes as he'd stared up at her from inside Cloud City's carbon-freezing chamber. And then of everything else they'd shared in the few weeks before that. How she'd begun to tremble when he'd taken her hand aboard the *Millennium Falcon*, drawing steadily closer until he'd finally kissed her. He'd been right about her—she did need a scoundrel in her life, someone who wouldn't salute her, who didn't care about her title or her role in the Alliance.

She wanted that someone to be him, but he'd been taken from her—like her adoptive father and mother had been, along with everyone else on her homeworld of Alderaan. She'd seen them die, incinerated by the Death Star's superlaser while Grand Moff Tarkin and Darth Vader forced her to watch. And now Han was gone, beyond her reach. All she could do was wait—in quiet desperation—for word from Lando Calrissian or Chewbacca.

Leia passed a cluster of rebel personnel crouched in front of an open door and had gone two steps past them when she realized none of the rebels had saluted— or even looked up at her.

She stopped, silencing C-3PO's complaints. One of the rebels looked up and she saw his face change as he recognized her. He started to come to attention, but she shook her head, staring down at the young woman on the repulsorcart in the corridor, at her shredded and blackened uniform.

"Oh," Threepio said. "Oh, my."

"What happened?" Leia asked.

"She was caught in the blast when the TIEs breached the hull, ma'am," the officer said. "We're stabilizing her here while the medical droids deal with those who are more badly wounded."

More badly wounded than this? Leia thought in dismay, looking at the gauze covering half the woman's face. The injured rebel saw who was looking at her and shakily lifted one bandaged arm, trying to salute.

"That's not . . ." Leia began, then stopped, remembering what Aymeric had said. The duty of the woman on the repulsorcart was to protect Leia, and she had paid a terrible price performing that duty. Leia could resent the special treatment, even find it appalling, but she couldn't let the injured young rebel see that. To make her think her sacrifice had been purposeless would dishonor her.

Leia fixed her eyes on the injured rebel's face. The woman grimaced, bringing her arm up farther, then let it fall, pain etched on her face. Leia nodded gravely at her, then at those around her. Then she hurried down the corridor and didn't stop until she was at the door to her quarters.

"I keep trying to tell you, Mistress Leia," C-3PO said. "I have a priority communication from Mon Mothma. We are to rendezvous with her and the rest of the Alliance leadership immediately."

"What? Why didn't you say so? Never mind. What's happened?"

"I'm afraid I don't know, Mistress Leia," C-3PO said. "All I know is we are to await transport once we come out of hyperspace."

CHAPTER 03
A FAMILIAR FACE

TO HER SURPRISE, Leia recognized the transport pilot waiting for her and the young, lean-faced rebel officer standing next to him.

"Nien!" she said, smiling at the dark-eyed Sullustan. Nien Nunb had pinned a rebel insignia to his worn flight jacket at a cockeyed angle, somehow finding a place for it amid the riot of patches already there.

Nien put his gloved hands on his hips in mock indignation.

"Escorting royalty!" he burbled in Sullustese. "If I'd known, I'd have charged the Alliance *twice* what I did. Lieutenant Ematt, I insist you get Mon Mothma on the comm. . . ."

"What nerve," sniffed C-3PO, standing behind Leia in the *Remembrance*'s airlock with her duffel bag. "Must everyone in this galaxy be a mercenary?"

"He's joking, Threepio," Leia said. Yes, Nien was a former smuggler—and talked as though he hadn't left that profession entirely behind—but he had risked his life to help Leia save Alderaanian exiles and preserve the destroyed planet's culture and heritage. She trusted him—and was glad to see him.

Her eyes turned to the officer next to Nien. She knew Ematt, as well—she'd once sent Han and Chewie to rescue him from the planet Cyrkon.

"Are you here to brief me?" she asked as the four of them crossed the docking bay to the *Mellcrawler*, Nien's cobbled-together star yacht. The chaos and clutter inside made the *Millennium Falcon* look like a spit-and-polish ship off the line.

"Afraid not, Princess," Ematt said. "The purpose of this trip is classified."

"Classified?" C-3PO said in disbelief, throwing his head back in a fashion that Leia knew all too well. "I'll have you know, sir, that Princess Leia safeguarded the plans to the Death—"

"Technically, Threepio, that information remains classified, as well," Leia said with a smile, enjoying the golden droid's horrified reaction. "Lieutenant Ematt's saying he doesn't know the reason for our trip himself."

"That's right," Ematt said.

"Can I at least know where we're going?" Leia asked, looking from Ematt to where Nien was scrutinizing a readout at the *Mellcrawler*'s engineering station.

"That's classified, too," Nien said, one corner of his mouth crooking upward. "Can't be too careful hauling around known revolutionaries and blabbermouth droids."

That set off C-3PO again. As the droid began lecturing Nien, the Sullustan locked down his engineering station and led them forward, chuckling at Threepio's lengthy objections to the term *blabbermouth.*

Leia smiled, too. Nien knew who she was, but he didn't treat her like a princess or a senator or a rebel leader. To him, she was just Leia—and it was a relief not to have to be more than that. Nien was odd in a way she liked, and encounters with odd but lovely people were too brief in that terrible war.

Ematt settled himself in the cockpit's navigator's chair, shaking his head at the maze of circuitry overhead. Leia saw the look and smiled, remembering how many times she'd been convinced the *Falcon* was held together with bonding tape and prayers.

Nien turned and stopped C-3PO before he entered the cockpit.

"Afraid there's only room for three," he said, spreading his arms apologetically. "You can plug in to the engineering station and keep the *Mellcrawler*'s droid brain company."

"Unless my photoreceptors are malfunctioning,

this cockpit appears to contain four chairs, Captain Nunb," said a puzzled Threepio.

"Right," Nien said. "But, um, that chair isn't properly grounded. Gives me a nasty shock every time I touch it. With your high-quality plating, we could have a superconducting event—blow up the ship. And I don't think you'd want that on your conscience, would you?"

"Oh! If you don't mind me saying so, Captain, a malfunction of that sort sounds like something a qualified starship engineer should investigate immediately."

"Excellent advice, Threepio—I'll do just that when we reach our destination," Nien said. "But for now, I'd suggest the engineering station. Hope you've got some good jokes for the *Mellcrawler*—she likes those. But keep 'em clean, okay?"

"I regret to inform you that I am not programmed for jokes," Threepio said.

"Truly? I never would have guessed."

"Don't be too hard on Threepio," Leia said after the droid had departed. "He means well."

"I'll make it up to him with the best oil bath the Alliance has to offer," Nien promised, strapping himself in to the pilot's seat and warming up the engines.

"At the risk of pulling rank, *now* can I know where we're going?" Leia asked.

"Zastiga," Nien said. "For what I gather is a very important meeting."

Leia glanced at Ematt, who nodded. Zastiga was a tumbledown trade world near the edge of the Outer Rim, on the fringes of the galaxy and rarely visited by the Empire.

As the *Mellcrawler* soared away from the *Remembrance*, Leia felt an odd tingling she'd experienced before and come to trust. It meant that she'd soon find herself doing something of critical importance for the Rebellion.

That meant no more standing around feeling useless on the bridge of a frigate. It meant *action*. And that was an even bigger relief than getting to talk with her old friend Nien.

CHAPTER 04

RESURRECTION OF EVIL

THE JOURNEY TO ZASTIGA was a long one, during which Leia's eagerness for action gave way to impatience and anxiety. Every hour the *Mellcrawler* spent hurtling deeper into the Outer Rim felt full of peril. She pictured Imperial Star Destroyers descending through the skies of worlds with rebel sympathies, bringing fire and death.

Lying in her bunk, she would imagine Han free of his carbonite prison, trying to summon a last brave show of defiance as the crime lord Jabba the Hutt sentenced him to death. Though of course he might already be dead. Or cast adrift in space, a speck of carbonite never to be found. Or worse. No cruelty was too inventive for Jabba.

As she stared into the gloom, other faces would come to her. She thought of the young woman lying in the corridor of the *Remembrance*. Where was she? Being treated in bacta? Or had she been more badly injured than her rebel comrades had thought? When the medical droid finally reached her, had it been too late?

She remembered the pilots she'd briefed back on Hoth, young men and women sent up two at a time into the teeth of lurking Star Destroyers. How many of them had died before reaching the rendezvous point?

She remembered the troopers aboard her blockade runner above Tatooine, hurrying to take up defensive positions against Darth Vader's stormtroopers. They'd had the grim, empty eyes of men who knew their lives had dwindled to the last few minutes.

And always there were the faces of her adoptive parents, Bail and Breha. They must have had some warning of the Death Star's arrival above Alderaan. The battle station hadn't fired immediately but had waited—waited so Governor Tarkin could try to extract information from Leia and torment her with her own helplessness.

What had her parents seen? A screen image captured by a defensive satellite? A fixed, bright star in the sky where no star should be?

And what had they done, there before the end? Had they tried to escape? Or simply waited, as bravely as they could, for the unimaginable to become reality?

Zastiga's heyday had come and gone when the Republic was young, and the planet was covered with eroded ruins, interrupted here and there by modern construction. Nien Nunb brought the *Mellcrawler* into the atmosphere, following a signal transmitted on an encrypted channel, and set the craft down with a final stutter of retrorockets.

In the docking bay, Luke Skywalker stood next to the barrel-shaped astromech droid R2-D2. Luke was wearing a rebel flight jacket over a black shirt and pants. He smiled at Leia, embracing her, but his eyes were grim and there were lines around his eyes and mouth that she'd never seen before. Not for the first time, she wondered what had happened to him in Cloud City, when he had confronted Darth Vader. Luke had lost his hand and his father's lightsaber, but she sensed he had lost more than that. Something had changed him, something he was keeping to himself.

"The others are assembled," Luke said, smiling as C-3PO and R2-D2 renewed their decades-long argument behind him and Leia. "The meeting can begin as soon as we arrive."

"Do you know what this is about?" Leia asked.

Luke shook his head. "All I know is it's something big. But I have the latest intelligence report on Han."

Leia looked eagerly at him, then away.

"What is it?" Luke asked, and she had a funny feeling that he was in her head, somehow—where she didn't want him to be right then.

"It's nothing," she said, not wanting to explain what she'd been wrestling with, the argument she'd been having with herself in the nights aboard the *Mellcrawler*. "So what is the news about Han?"

"It's from General Cracken's people," Luke said, referring to the intelligence chief's operatives, who worked in the galactic shadows to obtain information. "They have a confirmed sighting of Boba Fett's ship over Tatooine, and supposedly Fett's been paid and is doing more work for Jabba."

"And is Han . . . ?"

"Unclear," Luke said. "Lando is trying to gain access to Jabba's palace so we can know for sure."

Leia scowled at the mention of Lando. He'd betrayed them when she and Han had sought refuge on Cloud City, turning them over to Vader as part of a plan to trap Luke. Lando had explained that he'd had no choice—Vader had arrived before the *Falcon* and imperiled the freedom of Bespin's people. In the end, Lando had been pushed too far and risked his life to free Leia and Chewie from the Empire, but that had come too late to save Han.

"Lando's trying to make amends," Luke said gently. "You have to believe there's good in people."

"And what will that matter if Han is dead?" Leia snapped.

In the silence she was aware of Nien and Ematt behind them, trying not to listen.

"But we can't dwell on our personal sorrows," she said. "My duty—*our* duty—is to the Alliance. That has to be more important than anything else right now."

She felt Luke's eyes on her and could almost sense his surprise. She picked up her pace, putting distance between the two of them as they emerged from the docking-bay complex and into the forlorn streets of Zastiga.

"Leia, wait," Luke said, and she turned impatiently, hands on hips. She didn't want to talk about it. She *wasn't* going to talk about it.

"It's *this* way," Luke said, pointing and smiling apologetically.

The safe house was at the center of a warren of alleys, and no fewer than three teams of rebel operatives challenged them as they moved deeper into the maze. Leia nodded in approval when the operatives demanded passwords instead of assuming everything was all right because they recognized her and Luke. That way, if there was some threat the operatives couldn't see— such as a hidden blaster or hovering drone—Luke or Leia could signal the danger by giving an incorrect password.

The innermost chamber of the safe house was protected by massive walls and meter-thick doors that could withstand anything short of an orbital bombardment, yet swung open smoothly and silently. Luke, Ematt, Nien, and the droids came to a halt at the doorway.

Leia turned to Luke, puzzled.

"This is far as I go," he said. "The meeting's top clearance only."

"What? That's ridiculous."

"It's all right," Luke said. "I told Wedge that Nien and I would meet him for a discussion of reconnaissance tactics."

"Tactics, *hah*," sputtered Nien. "Antilles owes me a drink for saving his tail at Hagar Secundus. I've chased him halfway across the galaxy to collect. You can use one of those mind tricks in case he tries to wiggle free again."

"You see?" Luke asked Leia. "We have a lot to discuss. I'll see you later."

The second Leia stepped inside the room, she knew whatever had brought her there was of the utmost importance. On one side of the space stood a number of top admirals and generals—she recognized the grim, hatchet-faced Admiral Nantz and the green-skinned Duros Admiral Vassa, along with General Veertag and General Tantor.

On the other side of the room, the Alliance's top

leaders were standing together in an arc. General Cracken, the intelligence chief, was standing next to the careworn General Carlist Rieekan, who'd been in charge of the rebel defenses on Hoth—and whose immediate evacuation order had saved many lives. Next to Rieekan stood General Madine, a cocksure Corellian from the Alliance's special-operations wing. Beside them stood Admiral Ackbar, the salmon-colored, goggle-eyed Mon Calamari strategist who commanded the fleet.

And in the center of the arc of rebel leaders stood Mon Mothma herself—the slim, regal Alliance chancellor. Her service to the galaxy dated back to the Republic, when she'd been the senator from the Core World of Chandrila and an ally and friend of Bail Organa's. Mothma had continued to oppose Emperor Palpatine in the Imperial Senate while working in secret with Bail and others to forge scattered cells of resistance into a unified rebel movement.

Mothma greeted Leia with a smile. She held her head high and proud, and there was a deep intelligence behind her eyes. But sadness was etched in her face— the product of too many evils endured and friends lost.

"Admiral Ackbar," she said, "I'll let you begin."

Ackbar signaled to a technician in the corner of the room. The lights dimmed and a hologram shimmered to life. Leia stared at it in puzzlement. It was the Death Star, complete with the superlaser dish that reminded Leia of a vast, baleful eye. But huge chunks of the battle station were missing, with skeletal fingers of metal outlining the full sphere.

"I don't understand," Leia said. "Is this from Yavin?"

That was the site of the rebels' now-abandoned base. Had the Empire somehow rebuilt the battle station from the fragments left behind?

"It can't be," Admiral Massa said from where he stood on her left. "Commander Skywalker blew that thing to bits with a proton torpedo. It's space dust."

"An old holo, then," said General Madine. Leia nodded, annoyed that she couldn't figure out what she was looking at. Perhaps the Empire was trying once again to resurrect the superlaser technology, to build a new kind of planet-killing weapon?

She scanned the other rebel leaders' faces. From her experience as a diplomat and politician, she could immediately tell who had seen that holo before and who hadn't. Madine looked shocked, and Rieekan had his chin cupped in one hand. But Mothma, Ackbar, and Cracken were quietly waiting for the others to get over their surprise at what they were seeing.

"This footage was obtained by Bothan operatives less than a week ago," Ackbar said. "It's from

Endor—on the edge of civilized space. The Empire has begun construction on a second Death Star."

Leia looked at the military leaders around her. Their faces were grim masks. She felt like she was in a waking nightmare and barely registered the details Ackbar was providing.

Larger diameter. More powerful superlaser. Advanced specifications.

Leia knew the Alliance was in no shape to take on another Death Star. Yes, the rebels had gained allies in the fight against the Empire, but the fleet was dispersed—rather than battling the Empire for control of the galaxy's star systems, the rebels were simply trying to stay alive.

The first Death Star had taken decades to build, at astronomical cost in credits and resources and lives. By destroying it, the rebels had struck a powerful blow against the Imperial war machine. But the Emperor had simply constructed another one.

Against such enormous power and wealth, what chance did they have?

"So we destroy this one, too," Madine said.

"It won't be that easy," Cracken said, beginning to pace the room. A part of Leia wanted to laugh at the idea that what Luke had done at Yavin was easy. "The Empire will have eliminated the flaw that allowed Skywalker to destroy the first battle station."

"Agreed," Ackbar said. "If this new battle station is completed, it will be invulnerable to external attack."

"An infiltration team, then," Madine said. "My commandos are the best in the galaxy."

"I have no doubt that's true, Crix," said Mothma, then looked at Leia, her expression almost apologetic. "But even if we succeed, how many worlds will die before we do?"

Nobody wanted to answer that terrible question. Leia crossed her arms over her chest and closed her eyes. She felt cold and like she couldn't catch her breath, and for a moment she was back on the Death Star, peering over Tarkin's shoulder at her homeworld. She'd tried to lunge at Tarkin, only to have Darth Vader grab her shoulder and yank her back. He had held her pinned against his armor, the ghastly noise of his iron mask filling her ears while her world died.

Mothma let the silence hang over the room for several moments, staring up at the half-completed battle station. Then she held each of them in turn with her eyes.

"Admiral Ackbar is right," she said. "The Death Star isn't our only enemy—time is, as well. Our attack must come before the battle station is operational—or all will be lost."

CHAPTER 05
A JEDI IN WAITING

MON MOTHMA ENDED the meeting after swearing all the rebel leaders to secrecy, saying they would return the next day to review their strategic options.

Luke had returned from his tactics discussion and joined her for the walk back to their quarters. She found his presence reassuring, even though she knew he was worried by her grim expression. Leia wondered if he'd ask her what she'd learned, then realized he knew better. He would do his duty and wait to be informed by the Alliance's leadership.

Or maybe that wasn't it. Maybe Luke was still struggling with whatever happened to him on Cloud City.

Glancing at him, Leia felt something stir inside her. It was confusing—what she felt for Luke was so different from what she felt for Han. But it was powerful nonetheless—a connection she could sense somehow. She wondered if Luke felt it, too. He had once had feelings for her—at times, it had been painfully obvious—but she didn't sense that from him anymore. That was a relief, but she hoped he felt what she did—because he was one of her very few friends in the galaxy.

And yet they would soon be parted, too—returned to their respective ships to run and hide from the Empire that wanted them both dead. Dead or in captivity, to be paraded on the Holonet and derided as Separatists and criminals.

We'll see about that, she thought.

Luke turned at the door to his own quarters to say good-bye. But Leia put her hand on his shoulder.

"What are your orders? After this, I mean?" Leia asked.

"I expect I'll return to the *Redemption,*" Luke said, and a shadow seemed to cross his face. "Bound for nowhere in particular."

"Bound for nowhere at all," she said, her frustration boiling over.

"Mon Mothma's position is that—"

"I'm more than familiar with Mon Mothma's position," Leia snapped. "I don't need it explained to me."

She looked away, embarrassed by the hurt surprise on Luke's face. But he simply nodded and waited, and she was grateful to him for forgiving her with simple silence.

"I thought you'd say you've gone back to flying with the Red Squadron," she said after a moment.

Luke shook his head.

"It's Wedge's squadron now," he said. "It wouldn't be right to swoop in and take that away from him."

"But if you're not flying, then what are you doing?" Leia asked. The question came out more harshly than she'd intended, but Luke didn't take offense. Still, he looked uncomfortable.

"What I'm asked to do," Luke said. "But I need to return to my Jedi training. I have a promise to keep."

After Cloud City, Luke had told her of his time on a strange swamp world and the teacher he'd found there. It had sounded like something out of a fairy tale, a story a governess on Alderaan might have read her long before.

"Without your lightsaber?" Leia asked, wondering how he would train without the weapon of a Jedi.

Luke smiled, a bit sadly.

"Weapons and war don't make you a Jedi," he said. "I know that now."

"But we need you here," she said.

"I know," Luke said. "And I've kept putting off my departure because I was hoping for news of Han. But now I suppose we have to wait a little longer, until we know what's happening on Tatooine."

"Right," Leia said, not wanting to explain that she'd been talking about the Alliance, not Han.

"I'm trying to be more patient—that was part of my training," Luke said, then smiled. "I wouldn't exactly say I've mastered it."

She smiled back at him, thinking that patience had never been one of her strengths, either. But then Luke's expression turned serious again.

"What we all need is a little more time," he said.

"We'll never have enough of that—no one ever does," Leia said. "And the Empire's trying to take away the little time we do have by never giving us a moment's rest."

She paused.

"But maybe we can steal some."

"What do you mean?" Luke asked.

"I don't quite know yet—but I'm thinking," she said, then smiled at his expression. "Patience, remember?"

CHAPTER 06
OPERATION YELLOW MOON

LEIA SPENT THE EVENING poring over star charts and cross-referencing them with Alliance intel. She read reports about the Empire's fleet movements and economic interests, about demonstrations and anti-Imperial activities, sifting through possibilities until her mind was made up.

And then, mercifully, she slept more soundly than she had in weeks.

She woke up to C-3PO's familiar chatter, and for a moment she didn't know where she was—her ears missed the familiar hum of the various systems that kept a starship running. Then it all came back: the new Death Star and the plan she'd come up with, the one she intended to present to Mon Mothma and her fellow rebel leaders.

When Leia returned to the briefing room, Mothma

looked regal in a beautiful pale dress, with a silver band around her hair. But the others looked exhausted—Madine was clutching a cup of caf, Ackbar's skin was dull and splotchy, and the buttons on Cracken's tunic were misaligned.

It had obviously been a long night. She wondered if any of them had slept.

Mothma nodded, and Ackbar brought up the holo of the Death Star.

"While this second Death Star's main reactor is exposed, the battle station is vulnerable—no matter what structural changes the Empire has implemented," he said. "We're still analyzing the technical specifications, but either our small attack craft or fighters should be able to fly into the superstructure while our warships provide protection."

"The Empire will have its own defenses—we'll need a considerable task force," said Admiral Nantz.

Before Ackbar could speak, Admiral Massa was shaking his head.

"We could bring every capital ship we have to Endor and still not have the resources to defeat the Imperial starfleet," he said.

"That's not the objective," Ackbar growled. "We won't win the battle ship to ship. We'll win it by buying time for our fighters."

There it was again, Leia thought—time. It could be

the most precious resource in the galaxy—often unobtainable at any price.

"We've confirmed something else," Ackbar said. "The battle station is protected by an energy shield generated from the surface of the moon."

He swiveled one large eye in Madine's direction. "We've selected a strike team of commandos. Their mission will be to knock out the generator so our attack can proceed."

"They'll need to begin their operation before our fleet arrives," General Veertag said. "How will we get them there undetected?"

"We're looking to secure an Imperial transport," Madine said, and Leia had the impression the two were continuing a long-running argument. "As well as gathering intel on the Empire's security measures."

A Mon Calamari admiral Leia didn't know raised her hand. "Endor is so far from the main trade routes— where will our fleet assemble? And how do we keep the Empire from knowing we're coming?"

"To that question, at least, we have an answer," Ackbar said.

The Death Star disappeared, replaced by a map of the galaxy. As always, Leia was struck by the beauty of its spiral arms, brilliant white but shot through with blooms and tendrils of color, the signatures of nebulae and dust clouds where new stars were being born.

Red lines appeared on the spiral arms—the great trade routes that connected the galaxy's star systems. Ackbar gestured, and a red dot sprang into existence in a location Leia recognized: Sullust, the homeworld of Nien Nunb. Then another dot appeared, on the edge of the galaxy. A dotted blue line stretched between them.

"The Empire has used S-thread boosters to create and maintain a secret hyperspace route running from Sullust all the way to the galactic edge," Ackbar said. "It's called the Sanctuary Pipeline and is one of the Empire's most important military secrets. Fortunately, our agents discovered the navigational data that will allow us to use it, too."

The admirals were muttering. Leia knew what they were thinking. The cost of such a project was enough to bankrupt whole star systems.

But then what was money to a regime that could build multiple Death Stars?

"Sullust is an opportunity for us—we have contacts with its underground," Ackbar said. "Our armada will gather there. The commando team will go first, to bring down the battle station's shields. Then the fleet will travel down the Sanctuary Pipeline to Endor. Questions?"

"With the fleet so scattered, it will take time to gather enough capital ships and starfighter squadrons,"

Nantz said. "And during that time the Empire may discover what we're up to."

"What we need is a distraction," Leia said. "And I know what we can use."

"I was just thinking the same thing," Veertag said eagerly. "We plant false information about a new principal base—"

"Actually, that wasn't what I was thinking, General," Leia said. "At all."

"It's been a successful gambit before," Veertag objected.

"It won't be this time. The Empire would simply add whatever planet we chose to the list of places for its new Death Star to destroy. And we have to assume the Empire will hear rumors that we're gathering our forces. Our distraction should fit with that scenario and lead them to make the wrong conclusion."

The admirals and generals exchanged looks, and she could guess what they were thinking: *Who is this politician to tell us how to run a war?*

"I for one would like to hear what Princess Leia has in mind," General Rieekan said.

That quieted the others. Leia stepped up to the holoprojector.

"I'll take a ship and a small crew," she said, inputting commands. "We'll go here—the Corva sector. It's about as far away from Endor and Sullust as you can get without falling off the galactic disk."

A wide swath of space in the Outer Rim, on the other side of the galaxy from Endor and Sullust, began to blink. Leia tagged four stars with red dots.

"We'll make it look like a recruiting mission but drop beacons along the way, with messages sending any ships that respond to a rendezvous point," she said. "We'll start at Basteel and continue to Sesid and Jaresh, with the supposed rendezvous point here, at Galaan."

She tapped on the holoprojector and the fourth red dot swelled into an image of a greenish gas giant with a large yellow moon orbiting it.

"We'll use codes that we know the Empire's broken but that it thinks *we* think are still safe. Meanwhile, our real fleet will be assembling as far away from Corva sector as possible."

"Operation Yellow Moon," mused Rieekan.

"You see? We even have a name."

"The Empire has a limited presence in Corva sector," Cracken said. "After Yavin we considered that area for potential bases of operation and fleet rendezvous points."

"Which is exactly why I chose it," Leia said, and smiled when Cracken raised his eyebrows. "It makes the Empire more likely to believe Operation Yellow Moon is real."

"Any ships that did respond to the beacon would be in terrible danger," Mothma said. "How would we warn them?"

"We wouldn't," Cracken said, his mouth set in a grim line. "We *couldn't*. For Princess Leia's plan to work, its true nature would have to be kept secret from everyone except the people in this room."

"We'd sacrifice them?" Mothma asked.

"We're at war," Cracken said apologetically, aware of the chancellor's displeasure.

"I see," Mothma said.

"I think Princess Leia's plan could work," he said. "Any advantage we can seize is worth taking. And if one small ship can tie up sectors' worth of Imperial warships, I'll make that trade."

"I'll admit the plan has its merits," Mothma said. "But sending you, Leia, is out of the question."

"Why's that?" Leia asked, putting her hands on her hips.

"You're too valuable an asset to the Alliance for us to risk your safety."

"My value to the Alliance is what will attract the Empire's attention," Leia said. "Palpatine wants me in prison or dead, and I've slipped through his agents' fingers more than once. That makes me a prize worth hunting."

"At the risk of losing you?" Mothma asked. "It's a desperate move."

"These are desperate times," Leia said, looking at the faces of the admirals and generals, determined to make them see things her way. "Perhaps the most desperate we've ever faced. Risking me is what will make the plan work."

Mothma looked from Ackbar to Madine to Cracken. Leia watched the glances pass among them. The four of them knew one another well enough that they could tell what the others were thinking.

Eventually, all eyes turned the chancellor's way.

"I need to think about this more," Mothma said. "I don't like the idea of attracting people to our cause under false pretenses—or putting Princess Leia in danger for a wild bantha chase. But as General Cracken says, we should use every advantage we can get. I'll decide by morning; in the meantime, we need to plan the Endor mission."

Leia wanted to scream that they had to decide now. But she'd seen too many diplomatic agreements lost at the very end because someone pushed too hard. She forced herself to turn to Cracken, face impassive.

"What did you have in mind for your team, Princess?" he asked.

"A pilot, of course. Nien Nunb, if he'll go—and lend us his ship."

"A wise choice," Ackbar said. "Nunb can fly anything, in any conditions."

"I'll need a communications specialist," Leia said.

"I'd recommend Kidi Aleri," Cracken said. "She's adept at ferreting out signals and hiding messages within comm loops."

Leia nodded.

"I'd also suggest you take a tech specialist—a tinkerer, someone who can keep those beacons running. They're fickle pieces of machinery. I'm thinking Antrot, from my shop. He can hot-wire anything and is handy with demolitions."

"Sounds like I've got a crew," Leia said. They weren't there yet, but Cracken's approval clearly meant a lot to Mothma, and Ackbar would have said something if he disagreed with her plan.

"If we go ahead, I insist on one more addition to the crew," Mothma said. "A commando, for protection. Someone who'll get you home safe if all else fails."

"This isn't a combat mission," Leia said.

"You don't know what it may become. It's not negotiable, Leia."

Leia saw immediately that if she fought Mothma on that point she'd lose.

"Very well."

"General Madine?" Mothma asked. "Who would you recommend?"

"I'll go myself," the Corellian general said. "I'd just worry anyway."

But Ackbar shook his salmon-colored head, his wattles wiggling. "We need you here to plan the Endor infiltration mission. And before you suggest it, that goes for General Tantor, too."

"Major Lokmarcha, then," Madine said, "a veteran Dressellian resistance fighter. He's saved my life on several occasions."

"Here's hoping he won't have to save mine," Leia said. "Ideally, he'll go out of his mind with boredom aboard the *Mellcrawler*."

She was already making a checklist in her head of everything she had to do to begin Operation Yellow Moon. It was a daunting list, but she welcomed the work ahead. She didn't know if her mission would succeed, but she did know she wouldn't be standing on a bridge feeling useless. She'd be taking action—action that just might save the Alliance.

All she needed was for Mon Mothma to say yes.

CHAPTER 07
THE CHANCELLOR'S COUNSEL

LEIA HAD JUST FINISHED a simple dinner in her quarters when her door chime sounded. She wasn't surprised to find Mothma standing in the corridor.

"I hope I'm not disturbing you," the chancellor said.

"Of course not. I was expecting you, in fact. Would you like something? I'll get Threepio—"

"That's not necessary," Mothma said with a smile, and Leia saw the dark hollows under her eyes. "You're the one I wanted to see. Sit."

Most of the people in the galaxy who could tell Leia what to do and be instinctively obeyed were dead—but not all of them. She sat.

"Have you spoken to your crew?" Mothma asked.

"Yes," Leia said, knowing better than to ask if

that meant Mothma had approved the plan. "They all agreed to go, though Major Lokmarcha was reluctant. He feels like he's letting down his commando team."

"And are you satisfied with them?"

"I am," Leia said, then hesitated. "Antrot, he's . . . let's just say he's a little odd. But then I've never met a demolitions expert who wasn't."

"Neither have I," Mothma said. "I know you're waiting for my decision. But before I make it, I want to talk about you."

"Me?"

"Yes. I'm worried about you."

"So am I," Leia said. "I'm worried about all of us—you, me, the Alliance, the entire galaxy."

Mothma leaned forward, her gaze direct and unflinching.

"I've known you practically since the day Bail brought you home to Alderaan," Mothma said. "I watched you grow up. Tutored you before you joined the Senate. And I've seen you carry on Bail's work with the Alliance. He would have been so proud of you—of the leadership you showed at Yavin and at Hoth."

Mothma looked away, and for a moment she looked old—old and badly worn down.

"I've missed him these last two days," Mothma said. "But then I miss him every day. His advice and his perspective. But mostly his friendship."

"So do I," Leia said quietly, waiting. She knew Mothma hadn't come to talk about her father.

But what the older woman said next surprised her.

"You have feelings for Captain Solo," she said.

After a moment Leia nodded.

"I've read the intelligence reports," Mothma said. "We don't have the resources to mount a rescue mission to Tatooine—particularly not with the Empire expecting us to make such a move."

"I haven't asked for the Alliance to do that," Leia said sharply.

"I know you haven't—and I know you wouldn't," Mothma said. "But Captain Solo has many friends in the Alliance. Which is why I'd intended to propose such a mission myself."

Leia looked at her in surprise—and for a moment felt wild hope swell inside her. But then she saw the expression on Mothma's face.

"You said 'intended to.'"

"Such a mission would now be much more difficult," Mothma said. "As you've heard, our commandos are needed elsewhere. But 'much more difficult' isn't the same as 'impossible.' We have what General Cracken calls unconventional assets. Commander Skywalker is in a unique position at the moment. And then there's you."

Leia shook her head, annoyed that Mothma was

talking around something that concerned her so deeply—and surprised the chancellor seemed to be dangling the promise of a mission to save Han in front of her.

"Bribery isn't your style," she said, and from the look on the chancellor's face she knew immediately that she'd made a mistake.

"You're right, it isn't," Mothma said, eyes flashing. "I don't need to bribe you if I decide Operation Yellow Moon is a no go. My rank as chancellor of the Alliance to Restore the Republic allows me to do that."

Leia looked away. She wouldn't apologize, but she'd let Mothma decide where the conversation went next.

"I brought it up, Leia, because I'm not sure what you'd say if I offered you a place on a rescue mission to Tatooine. And that uncertainty is why I'm here."

Leia looked down at her hands, twisting them in her lap.

"My duty is to the Alliance," she said, relieved to hear her voice sound unwavering. "Not to Captain Solo."

"Ah," Mothma said. "And what about to yourself?"

Leia started to speak but then looked back down at her hands in her lap, forcing her emotions more deeply inside herself. When she looked up Mothma was simply waiting, a gentle smile on her face.

"Go on, Leia," she said.

"Before I got the call to come here, my convoy lost a blockade runner—the *Ranolfo*—to an Imperial patrol," Leia said. "And the *Remembrance* was damaged during the fighting, taking casualties."

Mothma said nothing.

"That convoy was assembled to protect me," Leia said. "Because I'm one of the leaders of the Alliance. Because I'm a symbol. And it's not the first time people have paid with their lives to protect me. I accept that—I accept it and I understand it. The least I can do, in return for that sacrifice, is dedicate myself fully to the Rebellion. Particularly now, given what we face."

Mothma said nothing. She simply waited with her hands folded. It was a diplomat's tactic, used when the people on the other side of the table were in the worse bargaining position, when talking would just dig them deeper into a hole.

But Leia was a diplomat, too. So she did what the people on the other side of the table didn't do enough: she stopped talking.

Mothma surrendered first, which made Leia feel both slightly satisfied and a bit guilty.

"Do you blame yourself for what happened to Alderaan?" Mothma asked quietly.

Leia looked at her in shock.

"How can you ask me that?" she managed.

"I wasn't aware there were things we couldn't ask each other," Mothma said, then leaned forward. "Let me tell you a bit of intel I decided not to include in today's briefing. Once the new Death Star is complete, the Emperor plans military operations to eliminate all opposition to his rule. Massive invasion fleets—larger than any seen in centuries—will advance on Mon Cala and Chandrila. Their mission will be to destroy all resistance, blockade both planets, and then wait for the Death Star to arrive. The destruction of both worlds, the Emperor feels, will provide an excellent object lesson for anyone who might oppose him."

Leia felt numb. It would be Alderaan all over again—except planets would die whenever the Emperor commanded it.

Now it was Mothma who needed a moment to get control of her emotions.

"For decades, many on Chandrila have begged me to stop opposing the Empire—because of the danger to my homeworld," she said. "If what Palpatine desires comes to pass—if his new Death Star is built and his invasion fleets fly—will Chandrila's fate be because of my actions?"

"Of course not," Leia said.

"I wish it were that simple," Mothma said. "It *will* be

because of me—but only because the Emperor is willing to destroy an entire planet for the opinions of one person. Which is monstrous. Monstrous and evil. And if we accept that—if we let ourselves be ruled by such twisted logic—we may as well surrender."

Mothma smiled, but her eyes were full of pain.

"At least that's what I tell myself during the day," she said. "But in the middle of the night? That's harder."

Leia started to say something, then stopped. How many times had she left her bunk to study intel because she feared sleep would bring another nightmare about Alderaan?

"You make the Alliance proud every day," Mothma said. "By representing our cause—and by doing your duty. But duty won't give you comfort, Leia—and you need that. We all do. The comfort of friends—and of love. You were Bail and Breha's greatest joy, Leia—the love you shared was what sustained them through the dark years. Don't deny yourself another chance at love because of what the Empire did to them. Don't give Palpatine that victory, too."

"I haven't," Leia said. "And I won't."

"I hope that's true," Mothma said. "Because it's the kind of battle you can lose without knowing it."

She got smoothly to her feet.

"Operation Yellow Moon is approved," she said, in

the tone Leia had worked so hard to imitate as a girl. "You're to tell me anything you need."

"Thank you," Leia said. "I promise I will."

"And you're to come back safe and sound," Mothma said, in a far quieter voice. "Losing you would be unbearable to me—to me and many others."

That's something I can't promise, Leia thought.

CHAPTER 08
THE TEAM ASSEMBLED

THE ALLIANCE MEETING broke up the next morning, with rebel officers slipping into Zastiga's many docking bays in twos or threes to leave the planet. Luke had to catch his own shuttle back to the *Redemption* but accompanied Leia to the *Mellcrawler* first. C-3PO and R2-D2 followed them, the protocol droid's baleful tales of slavers and pirates prowling Zastiga accompanied by derisive honks from Artoo.

In the docking bay several boxy power droids were ignoring Nien Nunb's orders, grumbling to themselves in their electronic language.

"Hey, we were supposed to be in space half an hour ago!" Nien yelled, hands on his hips in mock indignation. "I charge by the minute, you know—and there's no discount for royal titles!"

Leia waved that away and turned to Luke.

"I'll be back soon," she said. "Take care of yourself."

"You too," he said. "Be careful. And may the Force be with you."

"I'll take all the help I can get," Leia said, putting her arms around him. They stayed like that for a moment, taking comfort in each other, then parted. R2-D2 whistled mournfully.

"Speak for yourself," Threepio said. "I welcome the chance to avoid some ghastly peril for once."

Artoo hooted something rude.

"What a ridiculous sentiment. 'Adventures' is just a different name for 'terrible ideas.' "

Leia shook her head and hoisted her duffel bag onto her shoulder, leaving Luke and the droids behind.

"In fact, I charge nobility twice my usual rate, you know!" Nien yelled.

Leia was the last member of the crew to board the *Mellcrawler*—the others were waiting in the cramped lounge. She dropped her bag in the cabin she was sharing with Kidi—she'd refused Nien's repeated offers of his own single cabin—then emerged to find the rest of the crew waiting silently, their eyes on her.

"What I'm about to tell you is highly classified," she said. "Our mission has two objectives. I'll be meeting with local resistance leaders on three planets we're visiting. And we'll be recruiting ships to join us in a system we've given the code name Yellow Moon."

Kidi, the Cerean communications operator, nodded eagerly. She was thin and pale, with multiple pairs of headphones wrapped around her tall, conical head and datapads strapped to her spindly arms and legs. The datapads were blinking as data constantly flowed into them.

It pained Leia not to tell them that the rendezvous was a deception, but she'd spent the morning reminding herself that it was necessary. That way, if any of them were captured, Operation Yellow Moon would still fool the Empire, keeping its focus far from the fleet gathering at Sullust.

"In each of the three systems we visit, we'll set up a beacon designed to repeat a coded message," she said. "It will tell the starship captains we recruit the location of Yellow Moon and when to rendezvous with the ships we're committing to this operation."

Antrot, the tinkerer, looked up from checking the beacon in his lap. He was a member of the Abednedo species, with a knobby ridge atop his small black eyes. One of those eyes was magnified by a powered monocle.

If Leia felt bad about the story she was telling her crew, she felt worse about what could happen to any starship captains who responded to the beacon. Because there would be no rebel rendezvous—no fleet awaiting them. At best, there would be nothing but empty space, leaving the captains perplexed. And at worst? Imperial

Star Destroyers and TIE fighters might be waiting to disable or destroy them.

She swallowed at the thought, hating it, then steeled herself to go on.

As General Cracken said, we're at war, she told herself. *I hope we don't have to sacrifice any lives. But if we can save trillions of people elsewhere in the galaxy, isn't that an acceptable price to pay?*

"While we're in port, maintain operational security," she said. "Be careful who you talk to and what you say. There's no reason for the Empire to think we're anything but a private craft. But the Emperor has fleets, intelligence agents, and bounty hunters searching the galaxy for any sign of rebel activities. And Nien, Lokmarcha, and I are all wanted by the Empire."

Lokmarcha, the Dressellian commando, sat stockstill on the end of the acceleration couch, his wrinkled face expressionless, one hand lovingly tracing his blaster rifle.

"It's good to be wanted," Nien said in Sullustese, grinning. Kidi twisted a dial on her headphones, activating her translator unit, and asked him to repeat that. When he did, she nodded and smiled, then told Antrot. But the tinkerer just looked puzzled.

Leia wondered what they'd think if they knew Cracken's agents planned to seed various communications networks with rumors about their mission. It was strange to begin a mission by voluntarily endangering its secrecy, but it was necessary. Operation Yellow Moon would fail if the Empire captured them, but it would also fail if they did their jobs too well, attracting no Imperial attention.

"Any questions, come to me," Leia said. "All right then, at ease."

"One moment," Lokmarcha said, getting to his feet and standing beside her.

"I'm trained to spot threats and to terminate them," he said gruffly, his voice low and gravelly. "That means look to me and listen to what I say. It'll keep you alive. Got it? In a potential combat situation, I'm in charge."

"What's a potential combat—" Kidi began to ask, but Leia held up her hand.

"One moment, Major," she said. "I'm grateful to have you on this mission, but someone has given you incorrect information. *I'm* in charge—at all times and in all situations. No exceptions. Is that clear?"

The others nodded, but Lokmarcha was staring at her in shock. She held his yellow eyes with her own until he looked away, taking a sudden interest in cleaning a part of his gun that he'd just cleaned.

"It's clear," he said, hesitating a moment, *"Princess."*

"Good," she said, ignoring the emphasis he'd put on her title and turning to Nien. "And now, time to leave Zastiga behind. Let's see what the *Mellcrawler* can do, shall we?"

PART
TWO

CHAPTER 09
LIFE DURING WARTIME

LEIA DIDN'T HEAR the argument begin—she was in her cabin reviewing intel about their first stop, the planet Basteel. By the time she reached the *Mellcrawler*'s lounge, a red-faced Kidi was staring up at Lokmarcha, fists clenched. The Dressellian commando had his arms crossed and was grinning at the communications specialist.

"What's happening here?" Leia demanded, glancing over at Antrot where he sat at the *Mellcrawler*'s tech station, fiddling with a beacon's innards.

"Some kind of dispute," Antrot said. "I didn't hear any statements whose veracity I could assess, so I have been trying to ignore it."

"He's a monster!" Kidi said, her voice quavering, but Lokmarcha just grinned and shrugged.

"What happened?" Leia asked. "Kidi, you first."

"We were just talking. About how we wound up signing on with the Alliance. And this monster said—"

"Stop there," Leia said. "We're not referring to other members of this crew that way, no matter what they've said. Now try again, Kidi."

"I'm sorry, Princess. You're right. I told him how I'd been a signals analyst in the Imperial Survey Corps, before I deserted, and how I hope my former colleagues will get amnesty after we defeat the Empire. How the best way to have peace is to offer forgiveness. And he called me a, a—"

"I called her a naive conehead who'd been given one heart too many and one brain too few," Lokmarcha said. "I think that was it, anyway. I told her when we defeat the Empire we'll have mass trials—with most of her old colleagues going to prison or facing a firing squad."

His wrinkled face hardened and his eyes grew cold and reptilian. "Or at least that's what would happen if I were in charge."

"That's barbaric!" Kidi yelped, lapsing into silence when Leia held up a finger.

"So the two of you are arguing about how the Alliance should deal with Imperial war criminals," she said. "After we depose the Emperor, and defeat the Imperial starfleet and the Stormtrooper Corps, and dismantle the bureaucracy, and find and neutralize every moff, admiral, and general who refuses to disarm and keeps up the fight. Do I have that right? That's what you're arguing about?"

"Their argument didn't include a discussion of reconstruction efforts," Antrot objected.

"Do I have that *approximately* right?" Leia asked.

"*Approximately* is not a useful term," Antrot complained.

Kidi nodded, and Lokmarcha shrugged.

"I tell you what," Leia said. "When all those things have been accomplished, you two can argue about what to do next all you like. But since at the moment we're sharing space aboard one very small space yacht and hoping we reach Corva sector without being intercepted by about a thousand Imperial patrols, let's stick to the task at hand. Is that understood?"

Lokmarcha shrugged, but an embarrassed Kidi nodded repeatedly.

"I'm sorry, Princess," she said. "I never should have—"

"No need to apologize," Leia said. "Major, I have some intel I need to review with you in private. I'd appreciate it if we could do that right now."

She headed out of the lounge without looking to see if Lokmarcha was following her and was relieved to hear the sound of his boots a moment later. She waited for him to enter the cabin she shared with Kidi, then shut the door.

"I don't know what General Madine taught you as a commando, but I'm pretty sure what I just saw isn't the best way to build unit morale," she said instantly, hoping to keep Lokmarcha off guard.

The Dressellian just shrugged, a gesture that was beginning to irritate Leia.

"Kidi's a naive bleeding heart, Princess," he said. "Which means she'll freeze up when the shooting starts. Which means she'll *die*. I'm trying to toughen her up so that doesn't happen. After all, we're at war."

"We are," Leia said. "But Kidi can't do her job if she's constantly angry at another member of the team. So go easy, Major—that's an order. Can you follow that order? Or shall I ask Nien to divert to the nearest planet and put you on a commercial liner back to Zastiga?"

"No need for that, Princess," Lokmarcha said coolly. "Though I'd welcome it. My unit has a new Death Star to crack, back at Endor."

Leia looked at him in shock.

"What did you say?"

The Dressellian grinned.

"We'd already had our first briefing before Madine reassigned me," he said. "So I know the real mission.

We're a decoy, a diversion. You're wise not to let the others in on it—neither Kidi nor that scrap collector would last an hour under Imperial interrogation. Well done, Princess."

"You listen to me, Major," Leia said. "Not a word of this to anyone, under any circumstances. Or I'll have you before a court martial inside of a nanosecond."

That time Lokmarcha didn't shrug but just stared down at Leia.

"Back in the early days, before the Rebellion formally existed, a lot of guerrillas got their hands dirty doing things no one else wanted to do—or even think about," he said. "The Alliance would never have existed without them, Princess. Those men and women were my mentors—I've spent my entire career trying to live up to their example."

"Is there a reason for this history lesson, Major?"

"It's so you understand I'll take the secret to my grave," Lokmarcha said. "One thing you'll learn about me, Princess—I always do my duty."

CHAPTER 10
MISSION TO BASTEEL

"WELCOME TO BASTEEL," Nien said. "Never thought I'd be back on this rock."

Leia leaned forward in the copilot's seat. The planet below the *Mellcrawler* was small and gray. A scattering of ships—a motley collection of short-range freighters and boxy transports—were in orbit.

"Not exactly the garden spot of the Corva sector," she said.

"Corva doesn't have a garden spot," Lokmarcha grunted from the seat behind her, "just a bunch of compost heaps."

"Kidi, scan all rebel message frequencies to see if anyone's trying to contact us," Leia said. "And keep your ears open for Imperial traffic. The Empire garrisoned Basteel a few years ago in response to rumors of a resistance movement, but from what we've heard, it's a token presence. The thing to worry about is the TIE patrols. With any luck we'll be in and out before we have any trouble with them."

"Scanning now, Princess," Kidi said enthusiastically, her fingers a blur as they tapped at various datapads. Leia wondered how she kept track of what information she had on which device.

"Eladro City is the biggest settlement on the planet," Nien said as the *Mellcrawler* began to shimmy and bounce through the turbulent outer layers of Basteel's atmosphere. "Which isn't to say that it's big."

He took his hands off the controls and brought up a holographic representation of the planet, then zoomed in on the dot indicating Eladro City. The *Mellcrawler* lurched to port and Nien absentmindedly lifted his knee, bumping the control yoke to turn the little yacht back to starboard.

"Basteel's almost entirely mountain ranges—there's almost no flat ground and little vegetation," Nien said, tapping at the display as the *Mellcrawler* began to rattle and shake. "Eladro City's subterranean—a warren of tunnels carved out of the rock over the centuries."

"No flat ground? Where do we land?" Kidi asked, and Leia saw her fingers were white where they gripped her harness.

"Inside the mountains," Nien said, bumping the

Mellcrawler's controls again with his knee. "See this canyon—"

"Put your hands back on the controls!" Kidi said, unable to stand it any longer. "You can show me later!"

"Relax, Kidi—I'm a great pilot," Nien said. "I mean, nothing's killed me yet."

The Sullustan grinned, and Lokmarcha chuckled. Leia patted Kidi's shoulder soothingly. She knew Nien was a good pilot—and she'd endured enough flights with Han Solo that the approach to Eladro City seemed smooth and easy.

The cockpit door opened and Antrot entered, seemingly unconcerned about the bumpy ride. The Abednedo tech stood behind them with his arms folded over his chest.

"You'd better strap in," Kidi warned. "Our ship's being flown by a lunatic."

As if in response, the *Mellcrawler* bucked up and down in a sharp updraft. But Antrot stayed on his feet, not even uncrossing his arms. Leia peered at him. She hadn't expected the tech to have such good balance.

Antrot saw her questioning look and pointed at his feet. "I have customized my boots with magnetic soles."

"Customize my suit with magnetic everything, please," Kidi said.

"Relax—we're almost there," Nien said, steering the

Mellcrawler into a narrow canyon that looked as if some giant had created it by bringing an enormous ax down on Basteel's surface. In the canyon walls on either side, Leia saw mountain dwellings carved out of the rock, surrounded by intricate and beautiful designs.

Nien eased the *Mellcrawler* into a slot in the mountainside ahead, activating the yacht's floodlights. Antrot peered nervously out of the cockpit at the rocky ceiling a few meters above their heads.

"You didn't say we were going into a cave," he muttered. "I have claustrophobia."

"Then you've picked the wrong planet, pal," grunted Lokmarcha.

"It's actually quite roomy in here," Nien said as he peered down at a green-skinned alien waving glowing directional batons. "Plus it makes maintenance easier. The wind and ice do a number on any ships left out in the elements—up in the mountains your systems will freeze solid in a matter of days."

"I suppose that would be advantageous," Antrot said. "I hate rust even more than caves."

"There you go, then," Nien said. "Things are looking up already."

"My contact has a home deeper in the city," Leia said. "I think I've got the address figured out. I'll try to set up and activate our beacon as part of my meeting. Major, I want you with me. The rest of you stay with the ship—Kidi, monitor communications in case we have to make a quick getaway."

"Uh, about that, Princess . . ."

"What?" Leia asked, impatient with the Cerean tech's unwillingness to deliver bad news. "Out with it, Kidi."

"I know the codes for the Imperial military channels, but I can't pick up any transmissions. I can monitor comlinks but not exterior communications from ships or installations. It must be all this rock."

"Too much rock, and it's right over our heads," Antrot said unhappily.

"Relax, Antrot," Leia said, thinking that the landing pad was beautiful—its walls and ceiling had been carved into a dizzying array of shapes and reminded her of a cathedral. "That ceiling's been up there for centuries."

"Since comlinks work, do we have to stay with the ship?" Nien asked, his dark eyes hopeful. "I always get good intel in bars. Besides, I'm thirsty."

Kidi nodded eagerly. "Can we see the city?"

"We're not tourists, you know," grumbled Lokmarcha, which was enough to make up Leia's mind.

"You can take a look around," Leia said. "But stick together—and keep your comlinks handy."

She tossed Nien a handful of credits, which the Sullustan snapped out of the air.

"First drink's on me," she said. "You're buying the second one."

"And the third?"

"Don't have a third, flyboy."

Nien grinned and saluted.

As the group moved deeper through the tunnels of Eladro City, Leia told the others about her contact on Basteel. His name was Bon Yoth, and he'd once been a part of the Alliance but resigned his commission after a disagreement with General Rieekan. Rieekan hadn't told her what led them to part ways, but it had been clear that he was still upset about it years later. Still, he'd promised her, Yoth was no friend of the Empire.

Lokmarcha gave her a sidelong look and smirked, but that time everything she told them was true. It wasn't likely that Yoth could be brought back into the rebel fold, but it was worth trying.

And if Yoth paid the price for their having drawn the Empire to Corva sector? Leia hoped she wouldn't have to ask herself if that had been worth it or not.

The tunnels near the landing pad were wide, but kiosks built from plastic and reclaimed freight containers reduced the passage to a tight squeeze that left them bumping shoulders with everyone going the other direction. Lokmarcha had one hand on the butt of his holstered pistol, and Antrot was muttering in agitation at the cramped conditions.

"The bazaar's just ahead," Nien said. "I hope that four-armed bartender hasn't been pinched by bounty hunters. Guy made a mean Novanian grog."

"I hate these tunnels," Antrot said. "Only vermin live inside holes in the rock."

Many eyes turned their way.

"Maybe this would be a good time to keep your opinions to yourself," Leia said, edging closer to Lokmarcha.

Nien flung an arm around the Abednedo tinkerer with a companionable grin.

"I'll take you around my home tunnels on Sullust sometime," he said. "They make this look like a palace. Ah, here we are."

Antrot peered through his monocle at the maze of stalls, his distaste for caves momentarily forgotten.

"Oh!" he said. "Things!" And with that he took a hard left to pick through a vendor's collection of mechanical gear.

A crowd of aliens of multiple species gathered around the tinkerer, haggling loudly and enthusiastically. Leia stopped, concerned that Antrot might be in danger—or might react badly to being hemmed in by so many bodies. But then a cheer went up—Antrot had bought his first item—and soon he was being led to the next booth like a visiting dignitary, happily inspecting the strange piece of gear he'd acquired.

"He's fine," Nien said. "Kidi and I will keep an eye on him."

"All right," Leia said, but she couldn't help glancing over again as the Sullustan pilot and the Cerean communications specialist picked their way across the crowded chamber.

"We should go, Princess," Lokmarcha said.

"Something wrong?" Leia asked.

"I don't like crowds."

"Don't tell me you have a phobia, too."

She tried to keep her voice light, but the Dressellian looked grim, his yellow eyes scanning the crowd restlessly.

"Too many potential threats to keep track of," he said. "I swore to General Madine that I'd bring you back safe and sound."

"I'll be fine," Leia said, simultaneously annoyed by the commando's concern and impressed by his dedication to duty. "But you're right—let's keep moving."

At first no one responded when Leia banged on the metal door to Bon Yoth's house. She winced at how loud the clanging sounded in the narrow passages.

"We fly from one side of the galaxy to the other and he's not home?" she said. But then they heard footsteps, and the door opened a few centimeters, revealing a pale human face.

"Who are you?" the man asked suspiciously.

Leia drew herself up to her full height—which wasn't much, but she'd learned early that people who projected confidence and authority seemed much bigger than they actually were.

"Leia Organa," she said, "of the royal house of Alderaan. Carlist Rieekan told me where to find you."

"Oh, no," Yoth said. "Carlist and I parted ways a long time ago. You're not dragging me back into that madness."

Yoth tried to shut the door, but Lokmarcha jammed his foot against it. After a moment's struggle Yoth gave up and retreated. The room contained a scattering of furniture and a fireplace. Lokmarcha looked around suspiciously, then indicated to Leia that it was safe to enter.

Yoth was only a few years older than General Rieekan but thinner and paler, as though the lack of natural light had sapped something from him. But his eyes were sharp, and bright with anger.

"I'll tell you what I've told Carlist—no," Yoth said. "I'm done fighting the Empire. You're all kidding yourselves—no one can defeat the Imperial war machine. The best we can do is make our own communities better places while trying not to attract attention.

That's what I've done here. And it's made more of a difference than you'll make fighting your insane war."

"You're scared," Lokmarcha sneered.

"Quiet," Leia snapped.

But Yoth eyed the commando. "Of course I'm scared. If you're not, you're either a liar or a fool. So which is it?"

"I'm scared," Leia said quietly.

Yoth and Lokmarcha stopped glaring at each other and looked at her instead.

"I'm scared all the time," she said. "The Empire has so many warships and soldiers, and limitless credits. And what do we have? A ragtag fleet, not enough credits, and a bunch of fools. Fools like Major Lokmarcha and me who believe people should be able to live free of fear—and are willing to die to achieve that goal."

Lokmarcha nodded at her, smiling slightly. But Yoth looked unmoved.

"That's a stirring speech, young lady," he said. "But I said no and I meant no. I've made my decision, and I'd ask you and my old friend Carlist to respect it."

"Very well," Leia said. "General Rieekan thought you'd say that. So he had a different request for you. We need your help sending a message."

"What kind of message?" Yoth asked warily.

"This kind," said Leia, unzipping her bag and wrestling the beacon out of it.

Yoth looked suspiciously at the silver sphere she held. Leia handed it to him and he examined it, then pressed a recessed button on its equator. A small antenna emerged from the center and began to rotate.

"A hyper-transceiver," he grunted. "Haven't seen one of these in a while."

"But you know what it is," Leia said.

"Of course I know what it is, child."

Leia told herself to remain calm, giving Lokmarcha a warning look.

"What's the message?" Yoth asked.

"We're gathering starships at a rendezvous point in this sector," she said. "Looking for crews who'll support our cause."

"What rendezvous point?"

Leia weighed how to answer that one, aware of Lokmarcha's eyes on her. They wanted the Empire to find out about Operation Yellow Moon but not all at once.

"I think it's safer for you not to know that," she said.

"Fair enough."

"Now that you know what it is, can you tell us where we should place it? It has to be somewhere its transmissions can be received but the Empire won't find it for a few days at least."

Yoth pointed at the fireplace, where a few embers were still glowing feebly.

"I don't think that's going to work," Leia said. "The Empire would find it immediately."

Yoth laughed.

"Not in the fireplace," he said. "Up the chimney. It feeds into a network of vents and tunnels that eventually emerge among the peaks. Smugglers use them for dead drops. You can place it in the caves. But you'll need to get up a kilometer or so for the signal to reach the surface."

"A kilometer?" Leia asked doubtfully.

"It's not a tough climb," Yoth said. "Just takes a while. See for yourself."

Leia crouched on the hearth and opened the flue, ducking as soot rained down on her. The chimney was less than a meter wide, hacked out of rough stone that left plenty of handholds and toeholds.

She finished her inspection and turned to Lokmarcha, who had also crouched down to consider the route.

"How long do you think it will take to climb up and then back down?" Leia asked the Dressellian.

"Oh, no," Yoth said. "That's a one-way trip. You're not coming back here after placing that thing. You keep going all the way up and signal your ship to get you on the surface. We never saw each other, understand?"

Leia looked at Lokmarcha, who shrugged.

"Not my idea of a fun afternoon, but we can handle it."

"Except we'll need to take Kidi and Antrot up there with us," Leia said.

"All four of us?" Lokmarcha asked. "That seems dangerous. Kidi's brave, but she's a civilian. And the tinkerer will fall before we get ten meters up. Or panic and start foaming at the mouth like a Sparingian dire hound."

Leia shook her head. "I want Antrot because I'm not climbing up that little pipe and finding out the beacon's malfunctioned. And we need Kidi to enter the codes. Plus we might get to the top of the mountain and discover a comlink's not powerful enough to reach the *Mellcrawler*."

"They're not trained for this," Lokmarcha said unhappily.

"We'll all just have to do the best we can," Leia said. "Go find Kidi and Antrot in the bazaar and bring them back here. And tell Nien the plan."

Lokmarcha shrugged. "Your wish is my command, Princess."

CHAPTER 11
DWELLERS IN THE DARK

ANTROT REACTED WITH HORROR when they told him that they planned to ascend into the darkness above Bon Yoth's dwelling, but Kidi assured the tinkerer that it would be like climbing a ladder and promised she'd stay right with him.

"If the success of the mission depends on it, then I suppose I have to," Antrot said miserably.

"It might," Leia said. "Thank you, Antrot."

"I'll go first," Lokmarcha said. "Then the princess, then the tinkerer, and Kidi last."

"No," Leia said. "You lead and I'll take the rear. I've got more weapons and survival experience than Kidi or Antrot."

"But you're—" Lokmarcha began, then stopped and nodded. "No, you're right. Me, Antrot, Kidi, then you."

Lokmarcha strapped a lamp to the muzzle of his rifle with a length of bonding tape, then slung the weapon over his shoulder. He aimed the light up the hole, grunted unhappily, then shrugged.

"If anyone up there wants to take a shot at us they'll have a perfect target," he said. "But it's not like they'd miss in that small a space anyway. All right, let's go."

The Dressellian clambered up into the chimney and disappeared. Antrot had found a headlamp in one of his many pockets and secured it before following, with the bag carrying the beacon strapped to his back. Kidi went next, looking almost as miserable as the tinkerer.

"Good luck," Bon Yoth said.

Leia nodded and reached up into the chimney. It was loud in the enclosed space, and she could see Antrot's light moving back and forth, outlining Kidi's long arms and legs.

She reached up, feeling for handholds, and levered herself into the chimney until her toes found purchase. It was cool and dim inside, and narrow enough that she could rest by bracing her back against one side of the tube and pressing her feet against the other.

Long way to the top, though.

Bon Yoth closed the flue, leaving her in darkness. She looked up and saw Kidi a few meters above her. Higher up the chimney she made out the form of

Antrot, spotlighted by his headlamp when he peered down at them.

"We'll need a stable surface to set up the beacon," Leia called up to Lokmarcha, her voice echoing hugely in the shaft. "And we'll have to verify we're in communications range of the surface."

"Why not just set up the beacon on the mountaintop?" Kidi asked.

"Because the Empire will find it too quickly," Leia said, climbing after her. "Yoth said there was a warren of tunnels up above. We'll find a place."

"But what if he was wrong?" Antrot asked, breathing hard. "What if the tunnel gets too narrow? What if we get stuck?"

"Then we climb back down and blast him for lying to us," Lokmarcha said.

"That's no reason to shoot someone," Kidi said.

"Can you two not have this argument right now?" Leia asked. "Just keep going."

She quickly discovered the disadvantage of being last in line: every little bit of dust and rock dislodged by the others came raining down on her. It got in her eyes and nose, forcing her to stop and blink furiously. And she was all too aware of the drop below her. If she fell, she'd batter herself against the sides of the tunnel.

And the same thing would happen if one of the three people above her fell, she reminded herself as

Antrot slipped, catching himself only after kicking Kidi in the head. Leia was breathing hard now, her arms and legs were aching, and her fingertips were tender from scraping at the chimney walls and being stepped on by Kidi.

Everybody's tired, she told herself. *If you complain, Kidi and Antrot will lose heart. So keep going.*

"We're at an intersection," Lokmarcha called down to them.

About thirty meters above her, a low tunnel bisected the vent. Leia clambered up after the others, exhaling gratefully. The tunnel wasn't high enough for her to stand, but she was able to rest. Lokmarcha grinned while Kidi and Antrot just sat there, breathing hard.

"How far do the tunnels go?" Leia asked, peering past the others into the gloom.

"Farther than my lamp," Lokmarcha said, letting the light attached to his gun play along the walls of the rocky passageway. "Typical lava tube—"

"*Shhh,*" Leia said. "I heard something."

Kidi looked around fearfully while Antrot strained to see down the tunnel. Lokmarcha got on one knee, gun pointed into the darkness.

"It's your imagination," the Dressellian said.

"No, I hear it, too," Kidi said.

The sound was very faint—a distant, dry scrabbling.

Like claws on rock, Leia thought, trying to spot movement beyond Lokmarcha's light. Whatever was making that noise could see them perfectly well, she knew.

"I have a bad feeling about this," she said.

"Whatever that is, it doesn't have an A-280 rifle—or know how to use it," Lokmarcha said, patting his blaster. "Let's keep going."

"Go where?" Kidi asked.

"I did a little poking around while the rest of you were climbing. Yoth's chimney ends not far above us, but there's another down this way, and it goes all the way to the surface."

"How do you know that?" demanded Kidi.

"Because there's a gale blowing up into it," Lokmarcha said with his usual infuriating shrug. "And because I can see light at the top. It's pretty high, but we can make it."

"Oh," Kidi said, embarrassed.

"Kidi, see if you can get a transmission through this rock to the surface," Leia said. She couldn't hear that skittering noise any longer, but she didn't like being entombed in the dark heart of a mountain, knowing something cloaked in darkness might be creeping closer to them.

Her spirits sank when Kidi couldn't get any signals on her ship-to-surface receiver, but Lokmarcha suggested they try underneath the pipe he'd found. They crawled twenty meters down the low tunnel, the commando keeping his rifle aimed in front of him. As they went, the slight breeze steadily strengthened until it became a constant flow of air whistling past them.

Kidi adjusted a control on her receiver and gave Leia a thumbs-up.

"We can set up the beacon here," she said.

"There's even room," Leia said, relieved. Maybe it wouldn't be as bad as she'd feared.

Lokmarcha stood between Kidi and Antrot and whatever might be in the darkness, sweeping his light back and forth. Behind him, Antrot extended the beacon's tripod legs to keep it upright. He opened a panel on the orb's side and punched in the activation code, then turned to Kidi. She typed in a long string of numbers, then nodded.

"Got it," she said. "Signal is transmitting, alternating between Alliance codes Osk and Peth."

"Wait a minute," Lokmarcha said. "Did you enter those codes by hand?"

Kidi nodded. "I have all the Alliance encryption codes memorized."

"How is that possible?" Leia asked. "Each of them is dozens of random characters long."

Kidi shrugged. "I don't know. I just like numbers, I guess."

"It's also an enormous security risk," Lokmarcha said.

Kidi looked puzzled. "Why?"

"Because if you're captured the Empire will have all of those codes," the Dressellian said.

Kidi's face fell. "Oh. I never thought of that."

Lokmarcha shook his head, muttering.

"All right," Leia said, trying to stop another argument before it began. "It's not like Kidi can make herself forget them. Anyway, good work."

She peered into the pipe above them and saw a distant circle of white light. "The beacon will keep transmitting until the rendezvous?"

"I programmed it," Antrot grumbled. "That means it will work."

"Good," she said, peering into the darkness. "I'd like to get out of here, then."

Within a hundred meters Leia's fingers were hurting again. By then the problem wasn't just the rough-hewn walls but also the plunging temperature. Leia could see her breath, and her fingers and toes were numb. Above her, Kidi urged Antrot to keep going, assuring him it wasn't much farther. Leia wished she had someone below her to encourage her with little white lies—and to listen for things that might be crawling up the pipe after her.

"Watch out," Lokmarcha called down from above. "The rock up here is full of holes. We can still climb, though—and we're only about two hundred meters from the exit."

Leia stopped for a moment, her aching legs bracing her above the long drop into darkness. She tucked her hands into her armpits, trying to warm them. Her ears and nose were throbbing with cold.

"Princess?" Kidi called down. "Are you all right?"

Leia looked up and realized she'd fallen some thirty meters behind the Cerean.

"I'm fine," she said. "I'm coming."

She forced her aching limbs to move, climbing until she reached the area of broken rock Lokmarcha had mentioned. The walls looked as though they'd been drilled, and she thought the air was slightly warmer up there. Perhaps that was because of the sun she could see above. Or maybe it was just her imagination.

It also smelled funny—faintly of rot. And there was no way she was imagining that.

Go faster, she thought, reaching into the holes to get a better grip on the rock and climbing more quickly.

"Ow!" she said. She must have cut her finger inside one of the holes. It was hard to tell with her fingers so battered and numb.

She peered at the hurt finger, but it was too dark to

see. She stuck it in her mouth and the taste was sharp and coppery—blood.

Then something bit one of the fingers on her other hand. She pulled it back, twisting too far, and felt her body slipping. She flung out her hands and caught herself as she started to fall, one foot kicking wildly in the darkness, and clung to the wall, heart hammering in her chest.

"Princess?" Kidi called again.

"There's something alive down here," Leia said.

"What? Antrot, shine the light."

In the weak light from above, Leia saw malevolent red sparks glittering in the holes in the rock. They were below her now, too, forming a ring around the shaft. And she heard movement—tiny wet sounds that made the hairs on her neck stand up.

She began to climb, her movements growing frantic as the black shapes came boiling out of the walls. She could feel them on her hands, then her arms. And then they were everywhere—in her hair and on her face, moist and cold and slippery.

She cried out when something bit her ear. Then something else bit her hand. She could hear screams above her, too.

"Princess!" That was Lokmarcha. "Get out of the way, you two!"

"Don't fire!" Leia managed to yell. "You'll hit one of us!"

When she yelled one of the unseen creatures crawled into her mouth. Terrified that it would continue into her throat, she bit down, her teeth sinking through cold, wet rubbery skin. It tasted acidic and vile, and she spat it out, stomach heaving, the squelching sound of the swarm loud in her ears.

They were biting her everywhere then, and she shook her head violently, trying to dislodge them, but only smacked her head against the rock.

"Princess!" Lokmarcha yelled. "We're out! Come on! I can see you!"

She looked up and could see the others then, too, their heads silhouetted against a white circle of light. Panic drove her toward them. When she got within a meter of the top, the swarm stopped biting and scuttled away, seeking refuge in the crevices and holes lining the shaft.

They were afraid of the light, she realized. Probably night feeders that hid during the day.

Lokmarcha seized her arm and dragged her through the opening. She lay on the cold rock, gasping. Below her, countless eyes winked in the gloom and the walls of the shaft seemed to be in constant motion.

"Are you all right?" Lokmarcha asked, yellow eyes wide and staring.

"I think so," Leia said, hoping that was true. She sat up and looked around, hands exploring the bites on her face, dabbing at the little spots of blood left where the swarm had fed. The other members of the team were dotted with bites as well.

"What were those things?" Kidi whimpered.

"I don't know," Leia said, spitting to get the rest of the awful taste out of her mouth. "But if any tourists visit Basteel, I'd recommend they skip the chimney climb."

The shaft emerged in a low saddle between jagged mountains painted deep orange by the sunlight. It was freezing, so cold that the thin air was hard to breathe, and the wind was cruel, piercing their clothing.

"Kidi, tell Nien to come get us," Leia said. "We won't last long in these conditions."

The Cerean nodded, pulling out her comlink, then called for Nien.

There was no response.

"He better not be still hanging out in the bar," said Lokmarcha. He was shivering.

"He wouldn't do that," Leia said. "Keep trying, Kidi."

"Look!" Antrot said after Kidi had made four more unsuccessful attempts to raise Nien.

Leia followed the Abednedo's pointing finger and

saw three dots in the sky. They were far away, but she could swear they looked like . . .

"Find cover!" she said. "Get down!"

They scrambled into the sparse shelter of a boulder that had detached itself from the mountain ages before. A moment later the TIE fighters shrieked overhead, their solar panels winking in the sun.

"If we're captured, Princess, don't panic—I have a plan B," Lokmarcha said quietly to Leia. "One no one will ever find."

"I don't panic," Leia said. "But good to know, Major."

"Do you think the Imperials caught Nien?" Kidi asked.

"I hope not," Leia said. She was shivering, her teeth chattering uncontrollably. And, she realized, the sun was sinking toward the horizon.

Lokmarcha had seen it, too.

"We can't stay up here," he said grimly. "We have to climb back down."

"Past those things?" Kidi asked, her face gone pale with fright. "No. No way. I'd rather freeze to death."

"They're waiting till the sun goes down," Lokmarcha warned. "When night comes they'll emerge to feed."

Kidi shook her head, eyes fixed on the pipe from which they'd emerged.

"Kidi, *relax*," Leia said. "Panic won't help us. We

have to keep trying Nien. Now, does anybody have any survival gear? Anything that could help us?"

Lokmarcha shook his head. "I thought we'd only be out here for a couple of minutes."

"Kidi? Antrot?"

The tinkerer scowled, then brightened.

"I have a sheet of flexible insulation in my pack," he said. "It's for electronics—meant to keep heat out. But it will keep it in just as effectively. It works by preventing thermal radiation—"

"I don't need to know how it works right now," Leia said.

Antrot extracted a thin, metallic-looking sheet from one of his apparently infinite pockets. Unfolded, it was about two meters square.

"Give it to the princess," Lokmarcha said.

"Don't be ridiculous," she said, her teeth clacking together. "We'll share."

"It's not big enough for all four of us," Antrot said.

"So we'll shift positions," Leia said. "Twenty minutes at a time. Come on, huddle up. We'll need our body heat to stay warm."

She put her arms out, drawing Kidi and Antrot close and wrapping the insulated sheet around them, then inclining her head at Lokmarcha. He crouched a few centimeters away, clearly reluctant to come closer.

"It's not the Grand Coruscant Ball, Lok," Leia said, amused despite the desperate situation. "Come here, Major. That's an order."

The four of them clung together, the wind whipping at them. If it weren't so cold, Leia thought, she might have appreciated the view. The mountains were almost impossibly tall, their jagged peaks jabbing into the sky, and the colors were glorious.

They huddled together, shifting positions every twenty minutes, taking turns enduring the exposed space the sheet couldn't cover. At first Leia nervously watched the sinking sun, trying to figure out how long they had until it disappeared, and she ducked her head when TIE fighters passed overhead. But soon she was too numb and exhausted to care about either peril. She wondered if Han had felt like that as the liquid carbonite froze in place around him, forcing him into hibernation. She wondered if he dreamed in that state.

And if he did, was it of her?

She couldn't remember if it was time to tell Kidi to try contacting Nien again, or if they were supposed to rotate places. Her brain was skipping between random bits of memory—things that had happened so long before, on Alderaan and Coruscant and Bespin and other worlds. Planets that had been warm and full of life and noise.

Noise.

She forced herself to raise her head. The sun was low in the sky—opposite its fading glow, the first stars had appeared. The wind was a banshee wail, ceaseless and pitiless.

And a voice was leaking out of Kidi's headphones.

"Kidi!" Leia yelled, shaking the Cerean tech frantically. On Leia's other side, Antrot clutched her more tightly, moaning a complaint. Lokmarcha looked up, his yellow gaze dull.

After a moment Kidi's eyes snapped open. She looked at Leia reluctantly, uncomprehendingly. And then she heard the voice, too, and remembered what it meant.

"Nien!" she yelled into her headset. "Nien! I'm transmitting our position!"

Above them, a bright star was moving.

It was the *Mellcrawler*.

They were going to live.

CHAPTER 12
BROKEN CODES

LEIA HADN'T KNOWN that warming up could be so painful. The four of them lay in the *Mellcrawler*'s lounge, wrapped in slightly musty blankets Nien had found somewhere in the hold. They sipped soup from chipped mugs while the Sullustan fretted over them, asking if they wanted broth or tea or anything else.

"You should lie still and recover your strength, Princess," Lokmarcha said, huddled beneath a blanket on the other side of the acceleration couch.

"No, she shouldn't," Kidi protested. "She should sit up if she's ready. Keep the blood moving."

"I can tell we've survived because you two are bickering again," Leia said, and had to smile when both Kidi and Lokmarcha looked embarrassed.

Leia wondered what her aunts would say if they

could see her—filthy, half-frozen, and covered with bites. They'd probably lecture her about maintaining her appearance and the company she kept.

Ladies don't crawl up chimneys, she thought with a smile. *At least not in House Organa they don't.*

"Why did you not respond to our communications, Nien?" asked Antrot from where he was lying on the deck. "Were you still consuming the Novanian grog you remembered?"

"I wish," Nien said. "It was the Empire."

"I guessed that," Lokmarcha grumbled. "The TIE fighters were a giveaway."

"The Empire arrived with a landing craft," Nien said. "Stormtroopers fanned out and started searching the tunnels. The Imperials checked every ship's registration and captain's license. Fortunately for us, my documents were forged by the best slicers in the Outer Rim. But it still took forever. And then I couldn't raise you. . . ."

The Sullustan's ears drooped. Leia smiled at him.

"You did fine, Nien," she said, reaching up to squeeze his hand. "We're alive because of you."

"Well, I might have had something to do with it," Nien said with a smile. "Anyway, we're safely in hyperspace and heading for the Sesid system. And before we made the jump I did a frequency scan—the beacon was transmitting loud and clear."

"I don't understand, though," Kidi said. "Did the Empire just happen to be there? Or were they looking for us?"

Leia looked up to find Lokmarcha's eyes on her. She knew what he was thinking—that their plan was working. But was that true? Or was it a coincidence—some kind of crackdown that had nothing to do with them? No star system was truly beyond the Empire's reach.

She shoved the thought away—it wouldn't help them complete their mission.

"We can worry about it in the morning," she said. "For now, I suggest we get some sleep. It's been a very long day."

"That's an excellent idea," Lokmarcha said, getting to his feet and heading for the cabin he shared with Antrot. Then he turned and offered them a little bow.

"Good night, ladies and gentlemen," he said. "Don't let the hideous bugs in the walls bite."

Kidi stiffened. "That's not funny."

Lokmarcha shrugged, but he was grinning.

"All right, maybe it's a little funny," Kidi said.

In the morning, though, Kidi was in no mood for humor.

Leia was in the *Mellcrawler*'s cramped head, removing bacta micropatches from her face, when someone knocked at the door.

"I'll be out in a minute," she said, annoyed.

"Princess, I need to talk to you," Kidi replied. "It's urgent."

Leia heard no alarms, and the *Mellcrawler* was flying smoothly as it followed its course through hyperspace. She opened the door and peeked past Kidi down the corridor to the lounge. Antrot was fiddling with the innards of a beacon while Lokmarcha was sharpening a wicked-looking knife big enough to hold off a wampa.

Whatever was wrong, it wasn't an imminent threat to their lives. And that meant Leia could make a cup of caf first. She desperately needed one.

"Now then," she said a few minutes later, gratefully cradling the warm mug in her still raw hands. "What's wrong, Kidi?"

"Codes," Kidi said. "It's the codes!"

"I'm not following. *Kidi*. Take it slow. Tell me what's wrong."

"Antrot downloaded the codes Alliance Intelligence gave us to use during the mission," Kidi explained. "But when I saw the reports from Basteel, I got worried. So I checked the codes and they're ones we stopped using weeks ago, on suspicion that they'd been broken by Imperial slicers."

Over Kidi's shoulder, Leia saw Lokmarcha watching the conversation.

"I see," she said, stalling for time.

"I followed the orders that General Cracken's team gave me," Antrot said, looking more baffled than defensive.

"I'm not blaming you—it's *my* fault," Kidi said, her eyes wet. "I should have checked. And now I've put us in danger—us and anyone who hears our message. And everything that's happened on Basteel is my fault, too."

"Wait a minute," Leia said. "I missed when you said that earlier. What's happened on Basteel?"

"I saw it on an unauthorized holofeed this morning—there are still a lot of them operating in the Outer Rim," Kidi said. "I'll show you."

Nien emerged from the cockpit, looking as if he had something to tell them. But when he saw Kidi's agitation, he looked questioningly at Leia.

"She has something to show us," Leia said.

Kidi activated the holoprojector housed in the *Mellcrawler*'s engineering station. The report was breathlessly narrated, put together from footage shot around corners and from concealment. It showed Imperial officers in the tunnels of Basteel and stormtroopers holding people at gunpoint. Leia saw the blue rings of stun blasts. And then the report showed a line of beings—humans and aliens alike—being led in binders to a landing craft. She looked for Bon Yoth but didn't see him.

"Go back," Leia said. "Play it again. There—freeze that."

The hologram wavered slightly in the air. It showed a squad of stormtroopers and two officers. One was an older man, with gray hair and long sideburns. He was turning to look at the other officer, who was pointing.

The other officer was a woman. She was small and slight, about Leia's size, and wearing an olive-green uniform. Her mouth was a thin line, her gaze unflinching. She turned and Leia saw the rank badge on her chest.

"She's the one in charge," Leia said. "An Imperial captain."

Nien nodded. "That would be the commander of the Imperial Star Destroyer *Shieldmaiden*, then. I just got word from a former associate of mine. The *Shieldmaiden* arrived a couple of hours after we departed. Captain Khione is known for her dedication to duty, I'm told."

"A Star Destroyer on our trail already?" Leia said. "That's not good."

And yet that wasn't completely true. They needed their mission to attract Imperial attention. But that was a little more attention than she'd wanted.

"An Imperial crackdown will bring ruin to Basteel," Kidi said.

"Seemed pretty ruined already," Lokmarcha said, studying his reflection in his knife.

"You saw those people!" Kidi said. "They've got next to nothing and now the Imperial boot will be on their necks. And it's all my fault!"

Leia shook her head sadly. They'd been to only one world, and already that world was suffering from Imperial reprisals. And not because the Alliance planned to fight for the people's freedom, either. Those who called Basteel home were pawns in a larger game.

"Kidi, it's *not* your fault," Leia said. "Listen to me. I'm a prime target of the Empire. Anything could have happened—someone sighted me or a security drone saw us. We just have to keep going. If I'm a prime target, our best defense is to make sure I'm a moving target."

Kidi nodded uncertainly. "All right. Meanwhile, I can update our messages to use the latest Alliance codes. The ones we know are secure."

Lokmarcha stopped fussing with his knife, waiting to hear what Leia would say.

"We can't do that, Kidi," she said, hating the lie she was about to tell even as it came together in her mind. "We know the codes we're using may not be secure. But there hasn't been time for our agents to tell potential resistance movements about the new encryption keys. If you change the codes, the Empire won't hear our messages— but neither will the people we're trying to reach."

Kidi cocked her head at Leia. "But doesn't that put anyone who gets our message in greater danger?"

"Yes," Leia said. "But everyone we speak to and everyone we meet is in danger. And they will be until the Empire is just a memory."

CHAPTER 13

THE ISLES OF SESID

FROM SPACE, Sesid was a ball of brilliant blue, adorned with white swirls and flecked with black and green dots.

"It's a water world," Nien explained from the pilot's seat as the *Mellcrawler* descended. "Imperial corporations conduct pharmaceutical research here, and there's a garrison to protect those facilities. But most of the islands cater to tourists, and the local authorities want to keep them happy and spending credits. That means as long as we stay away from the pharma plants, we should be able to avoid any Imperial attention—stormtroopers tend to put a damper on a family vacation."

"And the resistance?" Kidi asked, turning to Leia. "Who are you meeting on Sesid?"

"All I know is his name is Aurelant," Leia said.

"He's some kind of local resistance leader. I'm supposed to meet him on a volcanic island slightly east of the main chain. Fortunately, we've identified the peak as an ideal place to set up our next beacon."

"In an active volcano?" Antrot asked, looking up from whatever he was doing. "I can accomplish a lot, Princess Leia, but molten rock is at a temperature outside of these beacons' range for safe operation."

Leia reminded herself to be patient with the quirky tinkerer.

"We're not going to throw the beacon into the mouth of the volcano, Antrot," she said. "We'll set it up on the slopes. And don't worry, the terrain data shows this climb will be a lot easier than Basteel."

"But the volcano is active?"

"Just a little smoke and the occasional rumble," Nien said with a yawn. "It hasn't actually erupted for, oh, five or six years."

Nien Nunb had been to hundreds of planets, but Sesid wasn't one of them, and he had to ask Sesid Traffic Control to repeat its instructions that he land the *Mellcrawler* on a giant leaf floating in the turquoise waters near the island called Thrinaka.

"We can accommodate a medium freighter, pal—the pad won't even budge with a little boat like yours," the tech on duty told Nien. "Rest easy and come enjoy a beautiful day."

Nien chuckled. "Never thought I'd be landing on a giant lily pad. Every time I think the galaxy can't get any stranger, it surprises me."

Kidi looked worried, but the *Mellcrawler* set down without incident, bobbing slightly on the massive, spongy leaf beneath it. The ramp lowered and humid air flowed into the space yacht. Leia blinked at the brilliant day outside and—unable to resist—spread her arms to feel as much of the warm sunshine as possible.

"So I like this place just a bit better than Basteel," said Lokmarcha.

"Me too," Nien said. "Think I'll come with you as far as town."

"You mean the first cantina, don't you?" asked Kidi.

"Your mission is climbing active volcanoes. Mine is gathering intel—and trying out a new tropical beverage or two. Either way, duty calls."

The fibrous veins of the giant pad made natural walkways, which the five of them followed to a pier. Birds wheeled in the sky, and Leia saw schools of fish moving as one in the shallow water, like peaceful miniature starfleets.

"This is lovely," Kidi said. "But how do we get to

the island where we're putting the beacon? Couldn't we have just landed there?"

"You always want to do it the easy way," Nien said with a grin. "Traffic Control would have spotted us immediately and alerted the Empire. Besides, this way you get to go boating."

They left the pier and walked along a broad board-walk of white wood, shot through with whorls of green and purple. Children of a hundred species were running around, pursued by parents, and multiarmed droids hawked everything from sweets to tubes of sun protection.

"What are those?" Kidi asked, pointing to clusters of tall black cylinders on the other side of the road. "They almost look like escape pods."

"That's exactly what they are," Nien said. "Every settlement here has them. In the event of a big eruption or seismic event, it's easier to evacuate people by launching them into space than it is to land and pick them up. There are big fines for using them in non-emergencies, of course."

Leia realized the Sullustan was eyeing them, one hand under his chin.

"What is it?"

"Your clothes. You can't rent a boat wearing that stuff."

"What's wrong with our clothes?" Kidi asked.

"You don't look like tourists," Nien said. "Which is fine, since we just arrived, but before long people will start asking questions."

Leia tried to weigh the perils of discovery against the need to keep the Empire on her trail. She decided—reluctantly—that Nien was right.

"Nobody told me to pack beachwear," Lokmarcha objected.

The Sullustan pilot chuckled. "Fortunately, Major, there isn't a beach town in the galaxy without people happy to sell you whatever you forgot to bring. Let's go get you properly outfitted."

"Nobody is to tell anybody about this, *ever*," Lokmarcha said. "I mean it."

Kidi tried to look serious but dissolved in giggles.

The Dressellian commando was wearing polarized eye lenses, purple shorts, and a T-shirt advertising a local smazzo quartet. His weapons and gear were confined to a duffel bag. He looked ridiculous, as well as furious.

He also no longer stood out among the throngs of vacationers walking along Thrinaka's boardwalk.

"None of us are exactly fit for military inspection, Major," Leia pointed out. She was wearing a flowered shirt that hurt her eyes over shorts, with a bright pink towel wrapped around her waist, having indignantly rejected Nien's roguish suggestion of a two-piece brown swimsuit adorned with gold braid. Kidi's tropical shirt was even more garish, and poor Antrot looked like he'd lost a bet, stumbling along with his eyes hidden behind oversize shades, and a cap bearing the logo of a local fishing charter sitting awkwardly on his head.

"I think you look great," Nien said. "We should stop so I can get a holo for Mon Mothma. . . ."

"No!" several members of the crew said at once.

But Leia was relieved when no one looked at them twice as they forked over an exorbitant number of credits to rent a repulsorcraft with a powerful engine. Nien waved from the shore as they waded out into the shallow water to where their boat was moored, surrounded by vacationers exchanging weather reports.

"The galaxy's at war and they're worried about an afternoon shower," grumbled Lokmarcha, up to his waist in water, with his duffel held over his head.

"I'm happy for them," Kidi said. "I mean, isn't that what we're fighting for? To make the galaxy a place where people are free to worry about silly things?"

"That's not the way I'd put it," said Lokmarcha, heaving his duffel into the boat. "But it's an interesting way of thinking about it."

"It is," Leia said. "Plus the water's nice."

"I don't like wide-open spaces," Antrot said. "I have agoraphobia."

"Oh, goodness me," Kidi said. "I feel like I finally have some room. Even a big starship gets to feeling cramped—particularly when you're a Cerean."

When they were aboard, Lokmarcha reeled in the anchor and they raced out of the lagoon and into the open sea, the boat flying over the surface of the water. The wind whipped at them, but unlike Basteel it was warm, full of the smell of salt and life, and Leia found herself smiling.

She was almost disappointed when she saw the conical island rising out of the water ahead of them. A thin plume of smoke trailed from its squared-off top.

"Our rendezvous point should be right in this cove," Lokmarcha said, cutting the throttle and easing the bow of their boat right up onto the beach.

"Pinpoint landing, Lok," Leia said. "Nien would be proud."

Lokmarcha gave Leia a small bow and they splashed ashore. The sand was black, littered with tiny white seashells—almost as if the night sky and the shore had switched places. Beyond the beach, the land rose steadily through green jungle to the steep sides of the volcanic cone.

Once on the beach, Lokmarcha turned serious again.

"I don't like sending those two off alone to set up the beacon—we don't know what kind of predators might live here," he told Leia in a low voice. "But I can't leave you alone to meet whoever this resistance leader is."

"You'll have to pick," Leia said. "But keep in mind that I can handle myself with a blaster, and they barely know which end is which."

"True. But my mission is to protect you, not them."

It was a simple statement of truth, but it still made Leia want to clench her fists. She was tired of people volunteering to die for her—because all too often they had to keep that vow.

"I have a comlink and you're not going far, Lok," Leia said. "If anything happens that I can't handle, I'll seek cover in the jungle."

The commando kicked at the black sand unhappily.

"Would it be better if I made it an order, Major?" she asked.

"It would be, actually."

Leia smiled. "Easy enough, then. Lok, I order you to protect Kidi and Antrot. And not to worry about me so much."

She watched the three of them cross the black sand with their gear and vanish into the green jungle. The waves broke softly on the beach, and the birds called overhead. It was strange to find herself somewhere so beautiful during such a terrible time.

But it was also comforting. Nature flourished even in a galaxy at war, creating life and beauty on billions of planets—beauty not even the Empire could eradicate. She sat down on the beach, watching the birds and trying to see how many species she could identify.

It was warm and there was no sign of a boat, or anything else that indicated her rendezvous was at hand. Leia decided to lie down for a few moments, to rest while she could. She rubbed her head back and forth in the black sand, creating a comfortable hollow, and stared up into the infinite blue sky.

And a moment later, she was asleep.

CHAPTER 14
AQUATIC PREDATORS

LEIA AWOKE WITH a start to see a figure standing over her, silhouetted against the sun. She scrambled for her blaster, knowing it was already too late.

"Relax, Princess—it's us," said Lokmarcha. "Fortunately for you."

"Leave her alone," Kidi said. "She was exhausted. It's good that she got to rest."

Leia got up hastily, embarrassed. The Dressellian commando was standing with Kidi and Antrot, looking out to sea.

"Is the beacon placed?" Leia asked.

"Transmitting perfectly," Kidi said. "Beautiful view from up there, too."

"But no one showed up for the rendezvous, I take it," Lokmarcha said.

"Not unless they decided to let me finish my nap and left."

She was relieved, actually—there was no need to endanger the mysterious Aurelant. With luck they could return to Thrinaka and head to their next destination, attracting Imperial attention without dire consequences for the people of this lovely planet.

"Let's get back," Leia said. "We have a schedule to keep."

They had just come in sight of Thrinaka when Leia's comlink began to chime.

"We're about twenty minutes away, Nien," she said.

"Turn around, then," Nien said. "There are stormtroopers in port—and the Imperial captain we saw on Basteel is with them. They're searching the town. I've got to take off in case they recognize the *Mellcrawler*."

"Lok, head back out to sea," Leia said. "Nien, you and Kidi figure out a comm channel you can use in case the Imperials start jamming us."

Lokmarcha cut hard to the left, sending their boat bouncing over the waves. Leia caught Antrot as he staggered across the deck.

"Don't your boots work?" Leia asked him.

"The deck material is not magnetic," Antrot said. "I believe it's wood. It would have been better if Nien had not rented such a fancy boat."

"Behind us," Lokmarcha said. "About five hundred meters. Electrobinoculars are in my gear bag."

After ordering Antrot to hold on more securely, Leia knelt and dug in the commando's bag. She braced herself against the boat's gunwale, grateful for the electrobinocs' stabilizer controls.

"Stormtroopers on waveskimmers!" Leia yelled over the wind. "And what looks like an amphibious transport behind them. Can we lose them?"

"Their boats are faster than ours!" Lokmarcha shouted back. "And out here there's nowhere to hide."

"Let me drive—we need you to shoot!" Leia said.

The boat hit a wave that sent it more than a meter into the air, repulsorlifts whining in protest. Leia landed awkwardly, pain shooting through her knees, and staggered across the deck before crashing into Lokmarcha's back.

"Don't let them get a bead on us, Princess," he said, scrambling across the deck toward his bag. Leia gunned the throttle and Lokmarcha slid toward the stern, smacking into it with his rifle already raised. He stared through the rifle sight and squeezed off a volley of blaster bolts at the pursuing waveskimmers.

"At this range if I hit anything it'll be dumb luck!" he said.

"Kidi, find something buoyant!" Leia yelled. "A

float-vest or chunk of insulation! Antrot, rig a detonator on a ten-second delay!"

She cut the boat hard to starboard, throwing up a sheet of water to spoil the Imperials' aim. Antrot was huddled in the bottom of the boat, looking queasy while rigging a detonator. The Abednedo's cap had flown off, and his sunglasses were askew. Blaster bolts sizzled in the water off to the boat's left, causing columns of steam to rise.

"Must be a deck gun on that transport!" Lokmarcha yelled. "Princess, hold our course!"

Leia risked a look behind her and saw Antrot holding a bright orange float-vest over his head. The tinkerer let go of it and it fluttered through the air, vanishing into the sea and then immediately bobbing to the surface.

Leia tried to count but lost track when she had to duck under a blaster bolt. She peeked over her shoulder just in time to see a column of fire erupt from the surface of the ocean. The black shape of a riderless waveskimmer skittered over the waves like a stone and then sank.

"Got one!" Lokmarcha yelled. "That was beautiful, Antrot!"

Then the bow lurched into the air and Leia felt heat on her back. The boat slewed crazily to starboard, and she briefly feared they'd capsize. She looked back and saw part of their stern had been vaporized. A thin ribbon of smoke began to trail behind them.

"We're all right—keep going!" Lokmarcha yelled.

The engine screeched as Leia tried to coax more speed from the damaged boat, which was listing slightly to port.

"This isn't going to work!" Leia yelled at Lokmarcha. "We need to head back to the island—the jungle will give us cover."

"Even if we beat them to the island, they'll only be a couple of minutes behind us!"

"Better that than anything that will happen to us out here! Kidi, monitor all channels in case they're coordinating with other units."

Kidi nodded, crouched over her own gear, as Lokmarcha fired wildly.

"I found their comm frequency," Kidi said, looking horrified. "That's Captain Khione back there—and they're looking for you, Princess. They used your name!"

"Never mind that, Kidi," Leia said. "See if you can raise Nien—maybe he can pick us up on the island."

Another blaster bolt set the water to port boiling. Leia began to juke the boat back and forth, listening nervously to the damaged repulsorlifts' protests. Black smoke was pouring from beneath the hull now. Antrot groaned and retched.

"There's something under our boat!" Kidi yelled.

Leia peeked over the side, hoping the Cerean tech was wrong, and saw a large dark shape below them. She cut the boat hard to starboard, flinging Lokmarcha to the deck. Antrot was lying in the bottom of the boat with his arms clutching his head.

Ahead of them, something rose out of the water.

It was a vehicle, she realized—huge and dark. A crack appeared in its blunt bow, widening until it yawned like a leviathan's mouth. Leia could see light inside and figures scurrying about.

Leia hesitated, then aimed for the mysterious craft.

"Princess, no!" Lokmarcha yelled. "We don't know who they are!"

"They're not shooting at us! Right now that's good enough for me!"

Another shot struck the portside of their boat and Leia ducked. Bolts zinged past them, kicking up sparks from the vehicle's hull. Leia saw that the ship was covered in lush green seaweed, like the shaggy coat of some massive animal.

The opening in the bow extended below the surface of the water, allowing Leia to zip inside without slowing down. She threw the engines into reverse, kicking up a column of water that soaked them. The basin inside the ship was ringed with catwalks, where humanoid aliens of a species Leia had never seen were gathered. They were human-sized, with silvery green skin, red eyes, and sharp teeth. They wore simple clothes and carried gear typical of sailors—along with blasters and knives.

Behind them, the ship's massive maw began to close. When Leia shut off the engines, the aliens began to cheer.

"I'm having trouble determining if we have been saved or captured," Antrot said weakly.

"Me too," Leia said.

One of the aliens directed Leia to bring the boat alongside a catwalk. When it drew within a meter, several of the aliens reached over and grabbed it, tying it fast with impressive speed and skill. Their fingers were long and ended in wicked-looking claws.

"Maybe we should have taken our chances with the stormtroopers," Kidi muttered as the pirates gestured with their rifles, ordering them out of the boat.

They took Lokmarcha's rifle away from him and patted down the others, laughing as a shaky Antrot had to be helped onto the catwalk. Pirates began pawing through their gear, holding up detonators and comm terminals and chattering excitedly.

The crowd parted and an alien a head taller than the others looked down at them. He was festooned with dozens of necklaces and bracelets, and his green arms were crowded with tattoos. A breastplate scavenged from stormtrooper armor protected his chest, and a heavy cutlass hung at his hip.

He grinned at them, his teeth brilliant white.

"Princess Leia Organa, I presume," he said in accented Basic, "of the Alliance to Restore the Republic. There's a considerable bounty on your pretty head, Your Highness."

CHAPTER 15
THE DRAEDAN PIRATES

LOKMARCHA STEPPED between Leia and the alien, teeth bared. But she pushed past the Dressellian commando.

"Don't," she whispered. "We're hopelessly outnumbered. Let me."

She eyed the alien pirates, hands on her hips.

"I see I need no introduction," she said. "But you do. With whom do I have the pleasure of speaking?"

The alien's grin got even bigger.

"Your captor," he said. "That's all you need to know for now."

The pirates laughed. Leia raised her voice to be heard above them.

"The Imperials will be here in moments—and then we'll all be captives," she said.

"We've already submerged—those fools will never find us down here. To off-worlders the ocean is surface and what lies beneath is mystery. The question is what to do with you, Princess."

"So we're negotiating?" Leia asked.

"Negotiating? Hardly. I'm thinking—you're waiting. Here's the thing, Princess—I'm a businessman. And you're worth a year's prizes, for a lot less risk. Can you offer me a deal that good?"

"You can have the boat!" Kidi said impetuously.

The pirates began to laugh.

"I already do," the leader said. "No, your offer will have to be better than that."

Leia tried to think of something she could use. She knew better than to promise the pirates a ransom from the Alliance. For one thing, the Alliance needed every credit for the fight against the Empire; for another, such a promise would just drive up the price.

"You're not friends of the Empire," she said.

"No self-respecting Draedan is," the pirate leader spat.

"So we have that in common."

Leia looked at the Draedan pirates, at their guns and their toothy grins. They were tough, and there was a darkness in them. But perhaps that wasn't all there was in them.

She'd have to hope so.

"I can offer you something better," she said. "A place in the Rebel Alliance. A chance to make the galaxy better. To fight not for credits or stolen goods but for freedom. Freedom for the Draedans and all the people of the galaxy."

"And what's that worth?" the pirate leader asked.

"More than anything," Leia said, then waited.

The leader cocked his green head at her, his red eyes narrowed. Then he laughed.

"You're fearless—particularly for a human," he said. "That's good. We had to know."

He made a curt gesture, and the pirates lowered their weapons.

"The name's Aurelant, Princess—Captain Aurelant," he said. "Welcome aboard the *Daggadol*."

Leia felt her shoulders slump in relief.

"You're our rebel contact?" Kidi asked in disbelief.

Aurelant nodded.

"We may be a small world, and far from the important places of the galaxy," he said, "but we have long memories. Memories of a time before the Empire, when Sesid was free and the stars offered possibilities, not threats. Perhaps Sesid can be that way again."

Leia bowed her head to Aurelant. The pirates began to cheer.

"You missed our rendezvous, Captain," she said.

"That I did," Aurelant said. "On account of the

Imperials. They've been prowling these waters for hours."

Leia felt her heart flutter, imagining if the Imperials had seen the boat in the cove and found one of the principal leaders of the Rebel Alliance by herself, asleep on the sand.

In a hideous flowered shirt, no less.

"Haven't seen an Imperial operation like today's on Sesid since the last time we Draedans went to war," Aurelant said. "They've locked down all transports off-world while they look for you. And there's a Star Destroyer in orbit."

"That's where we need to get, too—space," Leia said. "So we can continue our mission."

"Ah, yes. You—conehead. Can you tune a Horvax-16 transmitter?"

Kidi lifted her chin. "I learned to insert signals into the Holonet with a Horvax-8 when I was a kid."

"Did your Horvax-8 use a subaquatic amplifying array?"

Kidi shook her head meekly, but Antrot cleared his throat.

"I have made communications rigs function with everything from subaquatic amps to quantum relays. It's an easy customization."

"Good," said Aurelant. "That means the two of you probably won't damage our gear. I'd hate to get off on

the wrong foot by having to charge your Alliance for a replacement."

"Our ship's in orbit," Leia said. "But it's too risky to have it come down to get us—that Star Destroyer will blanket the area with TIEs."

"Rather than it coming to you, you go to it," Aurelant said. "In an escape pod."

"The Star Destroyer will see the launch. We'll be captured."

"Let me tell you something about Draedans, Princess," Aurelant said with a toothy grin. "I'm one of eighteen brothers and twenty-two sisters—which makes mine a shamefully small family. I have more cousins than I can count in every town within five hundred kilometers of here. The Imperials can target one escape pod, yes. But we're going to launch *hundreds*. They won't know which one is yours—but your ship will."

Leia smiled and nodded.

"You'll do that for us?" Kidi asked.

The pirates began to laugh again.

"What's so funny?" the Cerean asked.

"The Empire pays a salvage company to recondition accidentally launched pods and refuel them," Aurelant said. "One of my brothers owns that company. We won't make quite as many credits as we would turning your princess over to the Empire, but it will still be a pretty good payday."

CHAPTER 16
IN THE FIELDS

I N THE MORNING, on the way to the planet Jaresh, Leia's door chimed again.

That time, she wasn't surprised to find Kidi looking pale and anxious or to hear that the Empire had responded to Aurelant's escape-pod stunt with reprisals. The footage from Sesid showed nervous-looking tourists lining up for transports, stormtroopers escorting captive Draedans, and TIE bombers hurtling over the surface of the turquoise ocean, their angled solar wings sending sheets of water flying up behind them. In a transmission, the *Shieldmaiden's* Captain Khione demanded that all those who'd helped the rebel fugitives elude justice be turned over to the authorities—or all of Sesid would pay the price.

"Everyone who helps us suffers because of it," Kidi said, looking stricken.

"I know," Leia said. "That's how the Empire keeps people living in fear. By demonstrating that anything other than utter obedience brings brutality."

"But how can we ever stop such . . . such evil?" Kidi asked.

"By ridding the galaxy of those who commit such acts," Lokmarcha said. "You said 'evil' and you were right. There's no negotiating with people who would do that—or the far worse things done in the Emperor's name."

Kidi just nodded miserably, wrapping her long arms around her body. Leia felt like curling into a ball herself. Captain Aurelant and his pirates had seemed like marauders, but their reasons for opposing the Empire were as noble as any expressed by the people of Alderaan or Chandrila.

Now they would pay a terrible price for that opposition—and the Alliance would be no help to them. Leia knew perfectly well that the Rebellion wasn't coming to Corva sector anytime soon, not with the fate of the galaxy to be decided nearly a hundred thousand light-years away. The people of Sesid were alone—just as the people of Basteel were.

And as the people of Jaresh would be.

We're at war, Cracken had said, and Leia had accepted that. But now she wondered how much evil had been done, deliberately or not, because of that excuse.

Below the *Mellcrawler* hung the planet Jaresh, like a green jewel in space. As the yacht approached, Leia could see thin blue lines carved across the continents, marking a complex series of irrigation canals that brought water from enormous polar ice caps to the more temperate regions.

"It's quiet down there," Kidi said from beneath her headset. "I know there are communications towers that serve the planet, but you'd never know they existed if you listened. I've never heard a planet with that big a population and so little to say."

"Seems wise to me," Antrot muttered. "Maybe they save their words for when they matter."

"The first Jareshi colonists were part of a religious order," Nien said. "They've chosen to live with little besides basic technology and dedicate themselves to feeding nearby planets. Not my philosophy—I like my planets to be a bit more fun, thanks—but admirable enough, I suppose."

"We'll be landing near the village of Jowloon," Leia said. "My contact is there—a village matriarch named Nyessa. I'm to ask for her at the general store. As for our beacon, Alliance Intelligence suggests we install it at a communications node some twenty klicks outside of the village. How many of you know how to ride?"

Lokmarcha raised his hand. So did Kidi, though she looked tentative.

"I've ridden aryx," she explained. "Big bipedal birds native to Cerea. Do those count?"

"I don't know yet," Leia said. "Antrot?"

"I can ride in a speeder."

"That would be a no, then."

"What about you, Princess?" Lokmarcha asked skeptically. "Can you ride?"

"Former Alderaanian junior champion in steeplechase," Leia said.

"I didn't know that."

Leia shrugged. "It's rarely much use in space."

Nien set the *Mellcrawler* down in a spaceport that was little more than a landing field, a fuel depot, and a warehouse full of cargo containers. They stepped off the yacht to find the sun high in a bluish-purple sky dotted with white clouds. The air was humid and smelled of fertilizer.

"Well, it's not hard to figure out what they export here," Nien said. "Still, fertilizer's valuable. Maybe I can swing a deal."

"Better that than spending your time in the cantina," Kidi sniffed.

Nien offered her a little bow. "Don't step in anything."

He waved and headed back up the ramp. Leia, Lokmarcha, Antrot, and Kidi pulled their hats down and their cloaks closed, hoping to look unobtrusive as they walked through the muddy streets into the outskirts of Jowloon. The houses were made of wood, carefully maintained and painted. In the fields, farmers shouted encouragement to burly livestock of a species Leia didn't recognize—powerful beasts with bony plates on their backs, dragging plows behind them. Elsewhere, boys rested among herds of nerfs—though they weren't the Alderaanian breeds Leia remembered from her youth—or watched over whellays.

The crew of the *Mellcrawler* walked quietly through the village, but Leia still saw heads turn to note their passage.

Not a place where outsiders are common—or fail to attract attention.

Suddenly, Kidi stiffened.

"Look!" she said urgently, starting to lift her arm.

Lokmarcha pushed her hand back down.

"Don't," he said urgently. "Inconspicuous, remember?"

Leia saw what had attracted Kidi's attention—a pair of stormtroopers standing in the village square, their white armor a strange contrast to the rich colors around them, like blank spots in a painting.

"Keep going," she said. "They have no reason to be suspicious of us unless we give them one."

Jowloon's general store was like the rest of the village—simple and rustic. A few farmers were buying tools or feed while aged locals talked about the weather and finer points of animal care. Leia leaned her elbow on the counter and waited for the old woman behind it to look up inquiringly.

"I'm a friend of Nyessa's," Leia said. "She said I could call on her here. I've just arrived from off-world."

"Knew you lot was from away the second I saw you," the woman said. It wasn't an insult, just a fact she'd felt like stating. "This time of day you'd most likely find Nyessa by the warbu paddock."

"And where's that?"

"Same place 'tis always been—just up the hill from the ol' Galway farm."

Leia just waited.

"*Och*, that's right. You lot's from away. I'll make up a map."

Nyessa was a hunched, leathery-faced Kyuzo. She was ancient, but Leia saw a wiry strength in the way she held herself, and her eyes were brilliant yellow sparks beneath a broad-brimmed hat of gray felt.

"You'd be the ones from away," she said simply when they got her attention. "The rebels. Wait there a few ticks."

She called to the warbu—apparently, that was what the armored beasts were called—making a strange clucking noise. They eyed her from beneath their intimidating horns, then obediently plodded in the direction of a long shed with a water trough.

"Loyal beasts," Nyessa said with satisfaction. "Now then. I speak for the people of Jowloon. What 'tis that you need?"

Leia must have looked surprised, for Nyessa shook her head impatiently.

"Come now," she said. "I don't know how they do it out in the away, but on Jaresh we honor our obligation to help those who have pledged to help us. What 'tis that you need?"

Leia exchanged a look with Lokmarcha.

"Mounts," she said. "We have something—a machine—we need to attach to one of the communications towers, up in the hills. It's too far to walk."

"Just in time, then," Nyessa said. "A few more hours and the Empire would have fetched them to the corral to be tagged—urdas, warbu, nerfs, and whellays, everything. But I can lend you four urdas."

"The corral?" Kidi asked.

"'Tis newly built and on the other side of the village—you would not have seen it," Nyessa said. "The Empire wants to implement a system to track everything we have—beasts, crops, wells. So we can be more efficient in feeding their armies."

"Efficiency is helpful in every industry," said Antrot, looking puzzled when Leia shot him a poisonous look.

"You people from away want to change the way we are," Nyessa said. "We came to Jaresh centuries ago because we did not want to change. 'Tis that not our right?"

"Of course it is, Nyessa," Leia said. "And we want to restore that freedom. For you and everyone else in the galaxy."

" 'Tis good," she said. "But you must return by dusk."

Leia tried to calculate the distance to the communications tower and how long it would take to install the beacon.

"I assure you we'll take good care of the, um, urdas."

"That's not why," Nyessa said. "I need you back because tonight 'tis our meeting with the one who speaks for the Imperial garrison. And 'tis our obligation to tell him that his Empire is no longer welcome on Jaresh."

PART
THREE

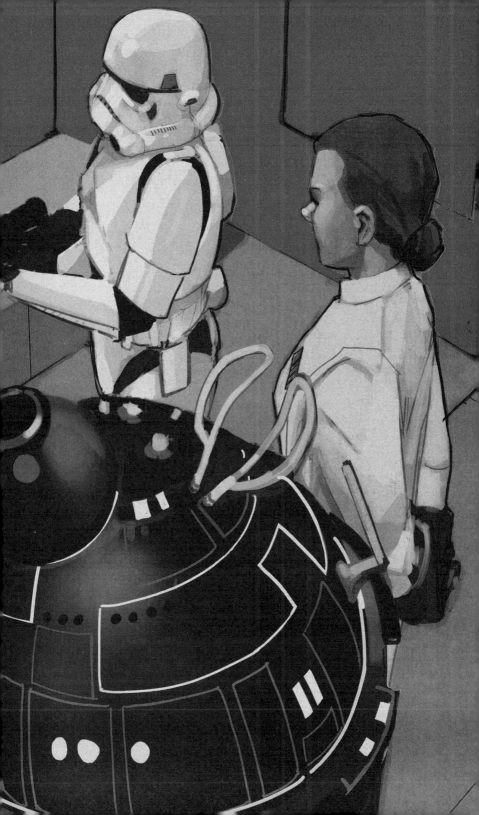

CHAPTER 17

A ROYAL DECISION

IT TOOK LEIA A MOMENT to stop gaping at Nyessa.

"You . . . you can't do that," she stammered. "They'll arrest you. Or worse."

"But you have pledged yourselves to us."

Leia looked at her helplessly.

"Yes," she said reluctantly, hating the lie. "We have. But we don't have the military forces to oppose the Empire here and now in that way."

"'Tis a disappointment," Nyessa said. "We had a covenant. But then you are from away. Anyhow, it does not matter. Our faith means obligations. Such as standing in opposition to evil."

"But you'll die!" Kidi said, aghast.

"Our obligation 'tis to do our duty. The consequences are not for us to determine. But now you must go. Come to the barn and select urdas to ride."

Urdas turned out to be long-legged quadrupeds with horny clawed feet and shaggy coats that smelled faintly sweet. After Kidi fell off hers for the third time, Leia told Nyessa that they would take only two of the mounts. They rode side by side, Antrot clinging to Leia while Kidi rode behind Lokmarcha.

The fields stretched for kilometers beyond Jowloon before giving way to low, scrubby forest crossed by a pitted road. Fortunately, the urdas were both sure-footed and smart, nimbly avoiding uneven terrain and obeying the slightest pressure from a knee or tug on the reins. Leia might have enjoyed the journey if not for the knowledge that Nyessa and her villagers planned to do something suicidal—and that Leia's arrival had led to that decision.

They began to climb into low, rounded hills, and soon after that Leia saw the communications tower ahead. They stopped beneath the massive structure, a metal lattice that stabbed a hundred meters into the sky like a spike.

"This mission involves too much climbing," Antrot said.

"Oh, come on, Antrot," Kidi said, setting her head-phones over her tympanic membranes and adjusting a control on a portable scanner. "Look—go up ten meters or so and there's a ladder. Easiest thing in the galaxy."

"The first time I climbed something on this mission, creatures bit me," the Abednedo tinkerer said. "The second time, I risked being incinerated by a volcano. If I climb up there, I will probably be hit by lightning or carried away by some avian predator."

"I don't think that's how logic works," Leia said.

"I am also tired and very sore."

The tinkerer handed the bag containing the beacon to Leia and walked away. He plopped down on the ground, extracting a piece of gear from one of his pockets and examining it through his monocle.

"But, Antrot, you'll miss all the fun," Kidi said. Then her face turned serious.

"What is it?" Leia asked.

"Now that I see it, this tower's a conduit, not a transmitter," Kidi said. "It passes along all the comm traffic from the network and pushes it out into space from an array on the other side of the planet."

"I thought you said this planet was quiet," Lokmarcha said.

"Compared to anyplace else it is. But we're still talking a planet's worth of messages. Our signal will get lost. We need to boost it, and that's tricky."

"But not for you," Lokmarcha said, giving her a fond smile. "You can do anything."

Kidi smiled back at the commando, then brightened.

"I know a way! A method for giving our signal a little extra shimmer. It'll take a little while, though."

And with that she picked up the bag containing the beacon, hooked a long leg over the lowest part of the tower's lattice, and began to climb.

Leia watched her go, but her mind was elsewhere. That odd feeling in the back of her mind was back. Something was about to happen, and she had a central role to play.

Leia tracked Kidi's progress, telling herself to relax, to trust herself. And then she knew what she had to do.

From Leia and Lokmarcha's vantage point, Kidi was a small figure against the sky, framed by the lattice of the tower. Lokmarcha watched the Cerean with a concerned look on his face, hands on his hips.

"Kidi knows what she's doing," Leia said. "Besides, I want to talk to you."

She eyed Antrot, but he was deeply involved with whatever he was fixing. Still, to keep the tinkerer from overhearing, she led the Dressellian commando over to where they'd tied up the urdas.

"I know what you're going to say, Princess," Lokmarcha said. "You're upset about the old woman and her crazy plan."

"Of course I am—and you should be, too."

"What can we do? You heard her—she's made up her mind. Anyway, the mission's been a success so far. You should be pleased."

" 'Pleased'?" Leia asked. "People on Basteel and Sesid are dead because we were there. And in a couple of hours, people on this planet will be dead, too. And all for a diversion. I didn't join the Rebellion for that— and I doubt you did, either."

"I joined it to defeat the Empire. Whatever the costs. We're—"

"Don't tell me we're at war, Major. Because if I hear that again, I'm going to strangle you."

Lokmarcha held up his hands peaceably. Leia fumed for a minute, studying Kidi at her work.

"Do we even need to make this final transmission before Yellow Moon?" she asked. "We know we have the Empire's attention—too much of it, even. We can go back and convince Nyessa to stand down, then tell any ships that have answered our call the same thing. . . ."

Lokmarcha was shaking his head. "We have the Empire's attention, Princess, but we need to *keep* it. Every day we can do that is another day for the fleet to assemble. And we both know everything depends on that."

Leia scowled, but the commando was right. She waited for Kidi to finish her work and test the beacon, trying to conceal her impatience. The Cerean tech gave them a thumbs-up, then descended. When she reached the ground, she was smiling.

"Plenty of shimmer," she said. "I just hope somebody hears it. We need all the allies we can get, right?"

Leia looked down at her boots, then back to the Cerean woman's beaming face.

"What is it, Princess?" Kidi asked. "Did I do something wrong?"

"No," Leia said. "You haven't done anything wrong."

"Princess, don't," Lokmarcha said.

"No, Lok. I've made up my mind. I can't do this anymore. Kidi, Antrot, it's time to tell you the real purpose of our mission."

She crossed her arms over her chest.

"Lok already knew—he'd been briefed before he joined our team," Leia said. "So I'll tell you two now, and Nien when we get back. And then you can decide what you want to do."

"I don't understand," Kidi said.

"You will," Leia said. "We're preparing for a major battle with the Empire—one on the other side of the galaxy from here. I can't tell you the reason for that battle—I'm sorry, I really can't—but we've been gathering our capital ships into an armada in preparation. The outcome of the battle could well decide the outcome of the war. If we lose, the Alliance dies."

"And so we're gathering new allies here, as well?" Kidi asked.

"No," Leia said. "Just listen to me. We're decoys. Or, more properly, I am—a moving target to keep the Empire's attention focused here. So that there's less of a chance they'll discover the location of our armada and strike before we're ready."

Antrot shrugged.

"Intelligence personnel always lie," he said, and went back to fiddling with his gear.

But Kidi's face was pale.

"That's why I was given old codes," she said. "The Empire already has them, doesn't it? The whole point was for them to sniff us out."

Leia just nodded. The Cerean had become a lot less naive in a hurry, she thought sadly.

"Which means you knew people on Basteel would die," Kidi said.

"No," Leia said. "I didn't know that. I hoped nothing like that would happen."

"But it did. And so you must have suspected it would happen again on Sesid."

"Yes," Leia said, forcing herself to meet Kidi's eyes, feeling as though she owed her that much.

"Those people died for nothing!" Kidi said.

"Not true," Lokmarcha interjected. "They died to help the larger plan succeed."

"That's terrible—" Kidi began.

"You're both right," Leia said. "The larger plan must succeed if we're to restore freedom to the galaxy. But it *is* terrible—and very hard to accept being a part of."

"Well, I don't accept it," Kidi said. "And I won't be a part of it any longer."

"I admire that," Leia said. "And I told you the truth because I'm not going to be a part of it any longer, either."

"It's too late! What can we possibly do to make amends?"

"I don't know if anything can do that," Leia said. "But I'm going to try. For starters, we're going to save Nyessa and the villagers of Jowloon. We're going to fight."

CHAPTER 18
WAR ON JARESH

THEY RETURNED to Jowloon in the late afternoon to find the streets strangely quiet. Leia couldn't figure out what was wrong for a moment. Then she realized the fields and pastures were empty of animals. The Imperials had taken them to the corral.

To Leia's relief, she didn't have to search for Nyessa—the old woman was hosing out her beasts' empty pen. She let her hands linger on the urdas' shaggy flanks for a long moment, comforted by their presence.

"We're going to get the rest of your animals back," Leia promised. "We're only four, but we'll keep our covenant with you."

" 'Tis no need. We will make our declaration and leave what follows to fate."

"I believe in making my own fate," Leia said. "Is there a barn overlooking the corral?"

"Yes. Old Grimshaw's."

"And can you trust him?"

"He is my cousin," Nyessa said. "But, yes, I can trust him."

"Excellent," Leia said, and then told Nyessa her plan.

"I suspect that I'm allergic to this vegetation," Antrot complained.

Leia wasn't particularly happy, either—the hay that filled Old Grimshaw's barn was dusty and itchy, and she feared one of them would sneeze and they'd be discovered. Only Lokmarcha seemed content. He had set up his blaster rifle on a tripod and was waiting patiently, occasionally peeking through the sight at the crowded square below.

"Do I need to go over the plan again?" Leia asked.

"No," said Lokmarcha. "Unless you're going to give me another chance to talk you out of it."

"I'm not. Antrot, you're sure the charge is set properly?"

"If I had any doubt, I would be down there eliminating that doubt."

"Good enough. We'll have to be patient, then."

Below them, the crowd had gathered, waiting for the head of the Imperial garrison to arrive. The crowd had left a space for the Imperials right in front of the gates of the corral, which was filled nearly to capacity with animals. Warbu lowed, nerfs and whellays bleated, and urdas nickered unhappily in the confined space.

"I see the Imperials now," Kidi said. "They're in a troop transport."

"What? Nyessa said they would walk."

"Well, she was wrong."

"If they park that thing in front of the corral our plan will fail," Leia said.

"We better hope they don't do that, then," Lokmarcha said.

The transport approached to within thirty meters of the edge of the square. Then twenty. Leia realized she was holding her breath. Ten.

Then the transport stopped. A dozen stormtroopers emerged, blasters holstered, and eyed the villagers from behind their skull-like helmets. Two Imperial officers were with them, hands behind their backs.

"I wish that Imperial captain were here, too," Leia said to Lokmarcha. "That's crazy, isn't it?"

"Very," Lokmarcha said. "At least she lost our trail."

The Imperials stood in front of the gate to the corral. One raised a loudhailer and ordered everyone to quiet down.

Little by little the crowd obeyed, until the only sounds were those made by the animals. Nyessa looked up and caught Leia's eye. The old woman nodded.

"People of Jowloon . . ." the Imperial officer began, his voice harsh over the loudhailer.

"Now," Leia said.

The charge Antrot had set behind the corral exploded, the light of the blast briefly illuminating the square. The animals shied away from it, shoving at one another, eyes rolling in panic. Nyessa was yelling, and the villagers were clearing the square as quickly as they could. The officers turned toward the corral, baffled.

Lokmarcha fired. The energy bolt from his rifle vaporized the lock on the corral. The frightened animals charged, shoving the gates open. For a moment Leia saw the stormtroopers and their officers in front of the corral trying to stay upright amid the stampede. Then they had fallen beneath the charging hooves and stamping feet.

But other Imperials had avoided the stampede.

"Take them out, Lok," she said. "I'm going down there."

The Dressellian looked up from his rifle, alarmed. "Princess, stay here where I can protect you!"

"If anyone comes near me, shoot them," Leia said over her shoulder as she pounded down the stairs.

She emerged from the barn into a chaotic scene—animals were rushing everywhere, eyes wild and hooves kicking. Some villagers were trying to calm the animals while others were simply trying to escape the fight.

A stormtrooper hurried around the side of the barn, clattering in his armor. Leia brought her blaster up and fired, leaving him in a heap. She saw other troopers' helmets turning her way as they shoved through the crowd, trying to reach the troop transport.

She couldn't let them get there.

Leia dodged a trio of frightened nerfs, ducking as a blaster bolt sizzled over her head. A warbu tossed its head, hooting angrily and eyeing a pair of stormtroopers in front of it. Leia smacked the beast in the hindquarters as hard as she could, shouting at it. Her hand went numb. The beast charged the troopers, flinging them aside. One scrambled to his feet, and Leia shot him. The other crashed into a crowd of villagers, whose fists rose and fell around the armored figure in their midst.

Two of the stormtroopers were back to back, firing into the crowd. Screams erupted around Leia. She looked up to catch Lokmarcha's eye—and saw a tall, coneheaded figure hurrying toward her, an E-11 blaster in her hands.

"Kidi! What are you doing?" Leia demanded.

"Fighting!" the Cerean replied.

A blaster bolt zipped between the two of them. Kidi aimed her gun at the stormtrooper who'd fired, but nothing happened. She stared at the weapon in dismay.

"Safety!" Leia yelled. A charging warbu knocked the trooper into her, spoiling both of their shots. The Imperial soldier grappled with Leia.

"It's too late for safety!" Kidi yelled at Leia. "We have to fight!"

"No—your blaster has a safety!" Leia yelled, struggling with the stormtrooper for control of her blaster. "To the left of the trigger!"

A grizzled villager brought a grain rake down on the stormtrooper's helmet, and the trooper crumpled. The villager grinned at Leia, then hurried away into the melee. Kidi fumbled with her gun, and a crimson energy bolt zipped past Leia's head and crashed into the side of the general store.

"Oh!" Kidi said. "Sorry!"

"Just stay behind me!" Leia said, yelling for the villagers to get out of her way. A blaster bolt zipped out from the barn, dropping another trooper. Lokmarcha fired again, forcing the troopers trying to reach their transport to duck.

Leia saw Nyessa in the middle of the square, ringed by brawny farmers. She caught the old woman's eye and gestured urgently at the troop transport. Nyessa looked that way and nodded, then began bawling out orders. A gang of villagers surged toward the troops, farm implements raised. The stormtroopers fired and two of their attackers fell—but the rest overwhelmed them.

It was over.

The square rapidly emptied of animals as they sought the pens and fields they called home. Kidi turned toward the corral, where the stampede had begun, but Leia steered her gently in the other direction.

"You don't want to see that," she said, leading the Cerean toward Nyessa instead.

"They are gone," the matriarch said with satisfaction.

"Yes," Leia said. "But they'll be back. And they'll punish your entire village."

"Perhaps," Nyessa said. "But a lot may happen before they get the chance of returning. Things can change. And if we die? It will be defending those we love and the things we value. There are worse fates."

Leia smiled at her. "There certainly are."

CHAPTER 19
WRATH OF THE *SHIELDMAIDEN*

NIEN NUNB HAD been busy. The hold of the *Mellcrawler* was filled with barrels of concentrated fertilizer from Jowloon—a cargo the Sullustan claimed would make him an enormous profit on Sullust.

Leia hoped so, because she could smell it from the lounge. Antrot looked stricken.

"Don't tell me you have a phobia about fertilizer, too," Kidi said with a grin.

"*I'm* gonna have one by the time I get off this ship," Lokmarcha muttered.

Antrot shook his head. "I have no phobia, though the smell is unpleasant. What concerns me is that this cargo is dangerously volatile."

Nien's face fell. Then he shrugged. "I'll try not to

fly into anything. Now, if you'll excuse me, I think it's time to get off this planet."

Leia was in the lounge, considering the best time to tell the Sullustan what she'd told the others, when the *Mellcrawler* lurched to starboard. Antrot's monocle popped off and Kidi clutched Lokmarcha, her eyes wide.

Leia raced to the cockpit, hands out to brace herself, and found Nien frantically flipping switches.

"Star Destroyer!" he yelled. "Snuck up on me from the dark side of the planet."

"It's the *Shieldmaiden*," Leia said grimly.

"Hang on! It'll take a minute or two to calculate the jump to hyperspace—gotta make it before they get a lock with the tractor beam!"

Kidi and Lokmarcha half fell into the cockpit. Kidi pointed at a light on the console.

"They're hailing us," she said.

Nien hit a switch with his fist and the cockpit was filled with a woman's voice, as cold as space.

"I am addressing Princess Leia Organa," Captain Khione said. "Shut down your engines and prepare for boarding—or the people of Jaresh will pay the price for your treason."

"Oh, no!" Kidi wailed.

"It's a bluff," Lokmarcha said. "They're not going to go after another target with us right here."

Nien adjusted his headset, ignoring Kidi's screams for him to fly the ship with both hands.

"Talk's cheap, lady," he told Khione, struggling with the unfamiliar sounds and rhythms of Basic. "You want us? Come get us!"

Alarms began to blare, and laser fire lit up space ahead of them.

"How long till you can make the jump?" Leia asked.

"I need another minute," Nien said.

"We don't have another minute!" Kidi yelped.

"Wait! Look on the scopes! That's perfect!"

A massive ship was ahead of them—judging by its profile it was one of the slow, colossal commercial vehicles that plodded between star systems.

"You're cutting it too close!" Lokmarcha warned.

"Let's hope not," Nien said. He headed straight for the massive freighter, juking and weaving to keep the *Shieldmaiden*'s tractor beam from locking on. Proximity warnings blared in the cockpit as the freighter's prow filled space ahead of them.

Then Nien dived below the giant ship, leveling out to streak along beneath its belly.

"Lock on to *that*!" he yelled triumphantly, then reached for the throttle. A moment later, the *Mellcrawler* shot into hyperspace and Nien threw his arms in the air, crowing.

"You're a maniac," Kidi moaned, hands still over her eyes.

"I know a certain Corellian who'd be jealous of that maneuver," Leia said, bending down to give the Sullustan a kiss on the cheek.

"So what happens now?" Kidi asked once Nien had appeared in the lounge to verify that the *Mellcrawler* had taken no damage and was on the correct course.

"We go to Yellow Moon," Leia said. "But the mission will be a little different than what we originally planned. Any ships responding to our beacons will be there in two days—but the Empire may be waiting. So as soon as they arrive we're going to tell them what our real mission was—and warn them to clear out."

"It's too risky, Princess," Lokmarcha said. "We've had too many close calls already. We've done what we came to this sector to do—we should get clear and set course for Sullust."

"Others are taking risks, too, Lok," Leia said. "Except they don't know what they're getting into. We have to help them."

"My mission is to—"

"I know what your mission is," Leia said. "And I'm grateful to you for your dedication. If any of you want to opt out of going to Yellow Moon, you've earned that right. I'll get Nien to find a safe port for you."

"I go where you go," Lokmarcha said. "You know that."

"I want to help," Kidi said. "Whatever the cost."

"I want to see if my beacons worked," Antrot said.

Nien chuckled.

"What can possibly be funny about this?" Kidi demanded

"Well, if I say no you have no ship."

"That's true," Leia said.

"No"—Nien grinned at the shocked surprise on Kidi's face—"way am I missing this."

"There's a problem, though," Lokmarcha said.

"Only one?" Leia asked.

"The Empire has the codes we've been using," the commando said. "If you broadcast an explanation, you'll also be telling any Imperial ship or spy droid that might be listening. And that could tip off the Empire about the real plan."

Leia stared at the deck, frustrated. "And we can't get a secure code to only the ships we want to talk to."

Lokmarcha nodded. But Kidi was smiling.

"I can," she said. "We send a new encryption code by tightbeam—ship to ship, not broadcast. I'd have to compress the code so it can be transmitted quickly, but I think I have time to do it. We only send the new code to the ships we want to hear it. Then we use that to encrypt your broadcast and we're talking only to our friends."

"And if one of them's a bounty hunter posing as a friend?" Lokmarcha asked.

"It's an acceptable risk," Leia said. "I'm not going to tell them everything, Major—I'm not *that* crazy. The Empire's not in the business of believing wild tales from bounty hunters. By the time they decide it isn't just more disinformation, the fleet should be assembled."

"A more immediate problem?" Nien began. "We don't know how many ships might be waiting for us. You may not have time to contact them one by one."

Kidi smiled.

"That's the value of having friends," she said. "We tell the captains to send my code along to those they came with. That way it only takes a couple of hops to spread the word to everyone."

Antrot looked up in puzzlement when Leia asked him to come into her cabin for a minute. Then he began packing up his seemingly infinite tools, one at a time.

"You don't need to do that," Leia said. "I just need you."

The Abednedo tinkerer obediently got up and followed her.

"What can I do, Princess?" he asked.

"Something secret," Leia said.

"There have been enough secrets on this mission already."

"You're right," Leia said. "I tell you what. It'll be up to you whether or not to keep this one. Fair enough?"

"I suppose."

"I want you to rig the ship," Leia said.

Antrot blinked at her. "To do what?"

"Explode."

"Our mission has had difficulties, but suicide seems like an overreaction."

Leia sighed. "I'm risking our lives contacting the ships responding to our call at Yellow Moon—but I'm also risking the future of the Alliance. If things go badly, I need a contingency—a plan B."

"Oh."

"What do you think?"

"How big an explosion do you need?"

"As big as you can give me."

"Not a problem," the tinkerer said. "Nien has the hold packed so full of fertilizer that there was a chance the ship would explode during our maneuvers over Jaresh."

"I was happier not knowing that, Antrot."

"My apologies," the tinkerer said. "People are always telling me that I've said too much or too little. It's confusing."

"I think you've done just fine, Antrot," Leia said. "And I'm grateful to you. So are you going to tell the others? It really is up to you."

Antrot thought about it for a moment.

"No," he said. "I don't know what Major Lokmarcha would say, but it would make Kidi nervous. And Nien would be angry. I think only you and I should know."

"All right then. Thank you, Antrot."

She opened the cabin door. Lokmarcha and Kidi were in each other's arms on the acceleration couch. Leia put a finger to her lips and gestured for Antrot to follow her down the corridor to the hold.

"Let's give them some privacy," she said, wrinkling her nose at the barrels of fertilizer around them.

"Why are they doing that?" Antrot asked, peering back down the corridor.

"Um . . ." Leia began, then realized she had no idea what to say next.

"I mean, they spent a large part of our journey arguing," the tinkerer said.

Leia smiled, thinking of an asteroid belt far away. For a moment she could almost see Han's eyes and the grin she'd found infuriating at first, then irresistible. Hadn't escaping from Hoth with a damaged hyperdrive been an impossible mission, too?

If I make it out of here, Han, I'm going on one more impossible

mission. Not for the Alliance—no matter what I'm told my duty is. But
for you.

"Princess?" Antrot asked. "Did you say something?"

"Oh, I was just remembering something funny. Sometimes arguments can be a way of hiding your true feelings, Antrot."

He shook his head. "That doesn't make any sense at all."

"You're right—it doesn't. But love often doesn't make sense."

CHAPTER 20
RENDEZVOUS AT YELLOW MOON

GALAAN HAD a strange beauty, Leia thought as she sat in the *Mellcrawler*'s cockpit. It was a massive gas giant whose bid to become a star had narrowly failed, leaving a glowing orb surrounded by a cloud of moons of all shapes and sizes. The largest was a sandy wasteland that reflected the yellow glow of its system's star like a mirror.

"Yellow Moon," Kidi said from the seat behind Nien. "It's hard to believe we're here at last."

"It is," Leia said. "How long until the rendezvous?"

"Less than an hour," Nien said. "And before you ask again, there isn't even a blip on the scopes. And no unusual comm traffic."

Kidi covered her mouth, looking embarrassed.

"What is it?" Lokmarcha asked.

"I was thinking that I really want ships to show up,"

Kidi said. "Because that would show that our mission succeeded. Our original mission, I mean. But that's crazy. Because it would be a lot better if nobody did."

They waited in silence. The appointed time of the rendezvous came, with no ships appearing. A minute passed. Then another.

"Maybe nobody's coming," Leia said hopefully.

An alert hooted on Nien's console.

"Ship coming in!" the Sullustan said. "Looks like a small freighter, but she accelerates like an attack ship."

"Ready with the new code?" Leia asked Kidi.

Kidi nodded, speaking urgently into her headset.

"They say they're the *Sapphire Rogue*, and they got our message at Sesid," she said. "Sending code now."

Then another ship came out of hyperspace, followed by another, and soon there were nearly two dozen, ranging from salvaged Clone Wars–era craft to space yachts like the *Mellcrawler*. Nien carved sweeping arcs through space to ensure Kidi could contact as many of the arriving ships as possible, seeding the code Leia would need. Kidi's long fingers flew over the keys of her datapads, but at last she looked up and smiled, giving them a thumbs-up.

"Let me have the comm," Leia said, then hesitated. She'd rehearsed what she was going to say half a dozen times but was still unhappy with it.

"All craft, this is Princess Leia Organa," she said. "I represent the Royal House of Alderaan and the Alliance to Restore the Republic. On behalf of the Alliance, we are honored that you have responded to our call."

"They're receiving," Kidi said.

Leia nodded.

"But please listen to what I have to say next," Leia said. "You are here as a small part of a larger plan—and I regret to say that has placed you in terrible danger.

"As I speak, a rebel armada is gathering to fight the Empire. What happens on that battlefield will determine the fate of the Alliance and whether our galaxy will be free once again. But we are not that armada, and this is not that battlefield.

"I brought you here to buy time for that mission. I brought you here under false pretenses. For that I am deeply sorry, and I swear I did so only because the Alliance was in grave peril. The call you responded to was a ruse, but my gratitude is very real. And so is that of everybody in the Alliance."

She swallowed.

"And now that you know the truth, I beg you—flee this system. Because my ship is being hunted. We kept our rendezvous to warn you, in case the hunters followed us here."

"Another ship coming in," Nien said.

"What kind is this one?" Kidi asked. "Nien? What's wrong?"

"It's an Imperial Star Destroyer."

CHAPTER 21
BELLY OF THE BEAST

NIEN MASHED DOWN the throttle and the *Mellcrawler* leapt forward, carving an arc across space, away from the ships that had answered the beacons' call.

"I outran her once—I can outrun her again," he said.

But this time they had no head start, and there was no bulk freighter to put between the *Mellcrawler* and the *Shieldmaiden*'s tractor beams. Leia knew they weren't going to make it, even before the *Mellcrawler* shuddered and slowed.

"If I don't shut down we'll get turned into scrap," Nien said apologetically.

"What about the other ships?" Leia asked. "Are they safe?"

"They're out of tractor range," Nien said. "And already jumping into hyperspace."

Leia looked back and saw that Antrot had something in his hand—a compact little device with two bright red buttons on top.

"Not until we're inside the *Shieldmaiden*'s belly," Leia said.

The tinkerer nodded.

"Inside?" Kidi asked, but Lokmarcha reached over and put his hand on Antrot's arm.

"Don't blow up the ship," he said. "We may still have a chance, Princess—I have my own plan B, remember?"

Nien looked back, his ears quivering. "Wait—you were going to blow up my ship?"

"Take the detonator apart," Lokmarcha told Antrot. "Hide the pieces in those pockets of yours. You can be plan C."

Leia nodded at Antrot.

"How did you know?" she asked Lokmarcha.

"The tinkerer and I share a cabin, remember? Antrot talks in his sleep."

Antrot looked chagrined. "I didn't know I did that."

"Besides, it's what I would have done," Lokmarcha said.

The *Shieldmaiden*'s shadow fell over the *Mellcrawler*, immersing it in darkness.

"I think it's time for you to tell me your plan B, Lok," Leia said.

The commando shook his head. "I'll be with you. You'll know. And if I've learned anything about you, it's that you'll find a way."

"Since you're not going to blow up my ship, I'll purge the logs," Nien said.

"Right," Leia said. "All of you, do the same with your datapads. Don't let the Imperials get any information except what's in our heads. And hang on to that as long as you can."

Antrot immediately left the cockpit. When Kidi got to her feet, her hands were shaking.

"They're going to interrogate us, aren't they?" she asked in a small voice.

"Yes," Leia said, and tried to push away memories of the torment she'd suffered at Darth Vader's hands, aboard the Death Star.

"Will it hurt?"

The question made Leia want to run and find Antrot and tell him to blow up the ship after all. But she steeled herself to remain in her seat.

"Yes, Kidi," she said. "I'm afraid it will."

When the stormtroopers led them down the ramp into the *Shieldmaiden*'s landing bay, Leia expected Captain

Khione to be waiting. But the officer at the foot of the ramp was a young lieutenant, who simply verified that they'd been disarmed and ordered them taken to a detention block.

"We haven't jumped to hyperspace," Nien whispered to Leia. "I would have felt it."

"They must be waiting in hopes of catching more ships," Leia replied grimly.

"No talking," a stormtrooper said, jabbing Leia in the small of the back with his rifle.

They threw Leia in a detention cell and shut the door. She scanned the cell in despair—it was the standard Imperial model, down to the hard slab of a bunk and the tiny pop-out washbasin. Her cell aboard the Death Star had been identical, and she'd come to know every centimeter of it.

I should have had Antrot blow the ship, she thought, hating the idea of Kidi's pleading with her captors, of Antrot's trying to reason with tormenters who would never listen. She hoped she wouldn't be able to hear their interrogations when they reached the worst parts, the ones that Leia remembered only in nightmares.

The light inside the detention cells never changed, so it was easy to lose track of time—a tactic the Empire used to disorient prisoners. But eventually the door to her cell slid into the wall and an officer walked in, two stormtroopers taking up positions in the corridor behind her.

"Princess Leia Organa," Captain Khione said. "We have a lot to discuss."

She tapped a button on a control unit attached to her belt. Leia heard an awful warble outside, and then the black bulb of an Imperial interrogation droid floated into the cell, moving with a slowness she remembered all too well. Her eyes inventoried its grim instruments—pincers and prods and needles. She knew them all, and how they were used.

"I'm impressed you do your own dirty work, Khione," Leia said. "Most captains would leave it to the Imperial Security Bureau."

"I enforce the Emperor's will in this sector," Khione said. "When things go wrong, I put them right myself. Anyone who knows my name ought to know that, too."

"Sorry to disappoint you, but until a few days ago I'd never heard your name," Leia said. "I'd barely heard of your sector."

Khione just smiled.

"Within a few days everyone in the Empire will know my name," she said. "But for now, it's your name that matters. And Kidi's, and Nien's, and Antrot's, and Lokmarcha's. We'll discuss them first, and then we'll move on to other names. Names of admirals, and starships, and planets."

"I'm not going to tell you anything," Leia said. "No matter what you do to me."

"Speaking of names, there's something I've always found interesting about this model of interrogation droid," Khione said. "It typically isn't programmed to know anything about a prisoner. All it knows is that you're the one in the cell—and that means you must be the interview subject. I've had prisoners break when no one's there to listen. They think they're talking to the droid, but it doesn't hear them. You can tell it anything and it doesn't care. It'll just keep working on you until someone tells it to stop."

And then, to Leia's surprise, Khione left, the door shutting behind her. The interrogation droid floated into the center of the cell, its repulsorlifts filling the enclosed space with that hideous cycling warble.

Leia jumped the first time it moved, expecting it to dart at her with one of its instruments raised. But it merely moved sideways and then began to hover again. She thought of attacking it but knew that would do no good. It would shock her, or retreat to the ceiling and summon the stormtroopers.

She sat down on the hard bunk, eyeing the droid. Her hands had begun to shake, she noticed, and she wedged them under her legs, angry at her loss of control. The droid extended one of its probes, and she instinctively retreated into the corner of the cell. Then the probe retracted and the droid was still again. Still and silent, except for the sound that was crawling little by little into her skull.

She wondered if Khione was watching. Watching and waiting for her to crack.

When the door opened Leia didn't know how much time had passed. Two stormtroopers entered, dragging Lokmarcha between them. He was in binders. His yellow eyes leapt to the black bulbous droid, and his hands began to shake.

Khione walked into the cell, her steps unhurried. It was all Leia could do not to spring at her. At a word from her, the stormtroopers exited the cell, leaving the door open behind them.

The Imperial captain wanted Kidi, Nien, and Antrot to be able to hear what would happen next, Leia realized.

"This one's admirably loyal," Khione said. "Promised to tell me everything if only I let him see his princess again first. But I don't think he has anything important to say. So we're going to do something else."

She smiled. "The droid's going to work on him, and you're going to watch. And then we'll repeat the procedure with the rest of your friends."

Khione touched the control unit on her belt, and the interrogation droid rotated away from Leia. It floated from side to side, scanning the room, then approached Lokmarcha.

The commando's yellow eyes turned to Leia and he nodded.

Lokmarcha's chest contracted so suddenly Leia heard his ribs crack. Then his chest expanded drastically, as if he'd taken an impossibly large breath. The hairs on Leia's arms rose as Lokmarcha slumped to the deck, already dead. The interrogation droid lurched to one side, dipped, then tried to rise. In the corridor outside, the stormtroopers clutched at their helmets, knees buckling.

Electromagnetic pulse, Leia realized. Lokmarcha had been carrying some kind of pulse bomb in his chest, one powerful enough to shut down a good chunk of a Star Destroyer. That had been his plan B.

Khione looked up in shock as Leia sprang at her. The captain raised her arms, but it was too late—Leia seized the interrogation droid, trying to get a grip on the machine's slick surface, and slammed it into Khione's head. The captain crumpled to the deck, unconscious, the interrogation droid lying motionless between her and Lokmarcha's body.

Leia looked sadly down at the Dressellian. She didn't want to think about what he'd endured to maneuver Khione into the only situation that would give Leia a chance.

I do have a chance—*thanks to you, Lok. And I'm not going to waste it.*

She hurried out of the cell, snatching a blaster from one of the fallen stormtroopers. Behind her, the lights in the cell flickered and died. She heard the cough and zing of blaster fire and ran down the corridor, stolen rifle raised.

A shape came toward her out of the darkness and she almost fired—then was glad she hadn't. It was Nien, holding a stormtrooper's blaster, with Antrot and Kidi behind him.

"The guards?" she asked.

"Not a problem anymore," Nien said grimly.

"Where's Lok?" Kidi asked frantically.

Leia shook her head sadly. Kidi stared at the floor and began to rock back and forth.

"He sacrificed himself for us," Leia said. "If we give into our grief now, he'll have done so for nothing. Antrot, do you still have your detonator?"

"I started putting it back together already," the Abednedo tinkerer said. "But it's not working because of the electromagnetic pulse."

"It will soon enough," Nien said.

"And so will everything else," Leia said. "We don't have much time."

The *Shieldmaiden* shook around them.

"What was that?" Kidi asked.

Leia looked at Nien and saw that he looked baffled, too. The Imperial warship shuddered again and klaxons began to blare.

"They're under attack!" Nien said. "If we can get to the docking bay—"

"We can and we will," Leia said. "I've got a plan. Nien, you and Kidi collect three pairs of binders from the guard station. Antrot, I need you to hot-wire a cell door. But wait here a minute—I need to change clothes."

She hurried back to her cell, stepping over the two stormtroopers, blaster raised in case either the droid or Khione showed signs of stirring. But both were still on the deck. One of the stormtroopers groaned and Leia stunned both of them, then fired a stun bolt into the fallen captain for good measure. Moving quickly, she stepped into the cell and set down the blaster, then stripped off her tunic and trousers before yanking Khione's uniform off. It was too big, and she tried to cram the extra material of the trousers into the tops of the boots.

The Star Destroyer shook again. Leia wondered who was attacking the Imperials. Had Mothma or Ackbar sent a task force after her?

She turned, adjusting Khione's cap, and saw Antrot standing in the doorway, looking uncomfortable.

"How long have you—oh, never mind," Leia said. "Shove the troopers in here and get the door locked. Quickly!"

"Does a minute count as quickly?" the tinkerer asked.

It didn't even take half that long. The door shut with a groan and a flash of sparking wires. Antrot gave her a thumbs-up.

Nien returned with Kidi and the items Leia had requested. Leia fit the binders loosely around her friends' wrists, checking to see that they appeared closed from a distance.

The *Shieldmaiden* shuddered again, and lights started to blink on in the detention block.

As they exited the detention level, Leia wondered if she heard a faint warble. Or perhaps it had only been her imagination, an illusion conjured by a wisp of unpleasant memory.

"It'll just work on you until someone tells it to stop," she murmured.

"What did you say?" Nien asked.

"Nothing. Come on."

CHAPTER 22
HEROES OF THE REBELLION

LEIA STRODE OUT of the detention block with the three cuffed prisoners beside her, her blaster rifle held waist high. Imperial officers and droids were hurrying along the corridor. They glanced at the gray Imperial uniform and her rank badge, but none of them stopped.

"Nien," Leia whispered. "I don't remember a Star Destroyer's layout."

"Straight a hundred meters or so, then take the elevator five levels down."

"Are you sure?"

"Sort of."

"Great," Leia said, then barked at them to move it.

They reached the elevator and found it guarded by two stormtroopers. Technicians were running around frantically, looking up each time the Star Destroyer shuddered around them.

The stormtroopers looked inquiringly at Leia and her prisoners.

"We lost power to the detention block," she said, trying to inject an icy chill in her voice. "These three are being moved so the interrogation can continue."

The stormtroopers nodded. One of them even summoned the elevator for her. Leia put a hand up in the face of a lieutenant who tried to get in with them, exhaling as the doors closed.

"Antrot, how's the detonator coming?"

"It would be easier without these cuffs," the tinkerer complained.

"What?" Leia saw, to her horror, that Antrot's binders were closed.

"Is something wrong?" the tinkerer asked, looking confused. "You forgot to close mine all the way, so I did it. I didn't want the Imperials to realize our subterfuge."

"Sweet dark-eyed mother of Sullust," muttered Nien.

"How are we going to get those off of you?" Leia asked, then shook her head. "Never mind. Just get that detonator working."

The lift doors opened and Leia gave a silent prayer of thanks that Nien had remembered his Imperial schematics accurately. They were in a broad corridor adjoining the *Shieldmaiden*'s docking bay, and she could see the *Mellcrawler* resting on its landing gear, perhaps fifty meters away. Not far from the yacht was a bat-winged Imperial shuttle with its ramp down.

"Go for the shuttle," Leia said. "Remember, we belong here. But you're prisoners, so don't go too fast. Ready?"

"Let's get going," Nien said.

"I'm ready," Kidi said.

"I think the detonator's working," Antrot said. "Though I won't know for sure until I push the button."

"We'll hope for the best," Leia said. "Let's go."

They marched into the docking bay.

"The magnetic shield's up," Nien said. "We won't be able to fly out of here unless it's lowered."

"One thing at a time," Leia said, prodding Nien with her blaster.

"Ow," the Sullustan complained. "First you try to blow up my ship and now you assault me."

"Keep talking and I really will assault you," Leia muttered.

"Princess Leia?" Antrot said, far too loudly. Kidi and Nien looked at him in horror.

"What is it, prisoner?" Leia snapped, hoping to remind the tinkerer of their roles.

"I rigged the *Mellcrawler* so the blast would hit the reactor and be directed outward through the engines.

If I blow it up in its current landing configuration, the blast will fill the docking bay. It'll do no hull damage to the Star Destroyer but extreme damage to everything inside this bay."

"Great," Leia said. "On to plan D, then. Or maybe it's plan E by now. Get on the shuttle, and I'll see if I can bully someone into opening the magnetic field."

"That's not going to work," Antrot muttered, looking distressed.

"Sure it will," Nien said. "Or at least . . . well, it *might*."

They were ten meters from the shuttle when a squad of stormtroopers caught sight of them.

"Ma'am, we're taking fire from rebel craft," the squad commander began, then stopped. "Wait. You're not—"

Leia shot him.

"Get on the shuttle!" she yelled as blaster bolts began flying.

Nien threw his binders in a stormtrooper's face and rushed up the ramp. Kidi followed, bashing her head painfully into the shuttle's undercarriage before finding her way. Leia fired at a stormtrooper before he could get a bead on her, then looked for Antrot—and found the Abednedo running the wrong way, wrists bound in front of him.

"*Antrot!*" she yelled. "*This way!*"

"Get on the shuttle!" the tinkerer yelled in reply.

Antrot hadn't made a mistake, she realized. He knew exactly what he was doing. They'd made a plan and he was going to carry it out. Now *he* was the moving target.

"Antrot, no!" she yelled, trying to think of what she could say that would make him turn around.

A blaster bolt caught the tinkerer in the arm and he stumbled, teeth gritted, but then ducked and rushed up the ramp of the *Mellcrawler*, which shut behind him.

"Leia!" Nien yelled from the shuttle. "We have to go!"

A blaster bolt struck near her feet and she smelled ozone. She hurried aboard the shuttle, the ramp starting to rise beneath her feet. Nien was in the pilot's seat, jabbing at the controls. Kidi sat behind him, fiddling with her headset. Then her hand went to her mouth.

"There's another Star Destroyer coming out of hyperspace!" she said.

"One thing at a time, right?" Nien asked.

"Right," Leia said. "Can you fly one of these?"

"I can fly anything. But it won't matter if Antrot's plan doesn't work."

Stormtroopers were firing at them from the floor of the docking bay. Their shots splashed harmlessly off the shuttle's viewports. Nien activated the repulsorlifts and the craft rose into the air with a whine.

"Poor Antrot," Kidi said, and Leia put her hand on the Cerean tech's shoulder.

"I need you on the comm, Kidi," she said. "Rebel frequencies—let whoever's attacking this ship know we're a friendly."

"Good thing I have those frequencies memorized," Kidi said.

The *Mellcrawler* lifted off the deck, moving sluggishly, then made an awkward turn and tipped downward. Its landing gear scraped across the deck.

"That lunatic's going to damage my ship," Nien complained as the yacht began to rotate clumsily.

Leia just stared at the *Mellcrawler* in dismay, imagining Antrot trying to guide the yacht with a wounded arm and bound hands. The tinkerer was stubborn and odd, but he was also incredibly brave.

"Strap in," Nien said. "This is about to get bumpy."

The yacht kept rotating until its engines were pointed at the wall of the docking bay, its bow facing the shuttle. Leia thought she saw the slim figure of Antrot in the cockpit in the split second before the flash polarized the shuttle's viewports and the bay filled with fire and noise.

Leia opened her eyes. Bright spots danced across her vision. She couldn't see, but apparently Nien could. He stomped on the shuttle's throttle and the bat-winged ship swooped through the gaping hole punched in the *Shieldmaiden*'s hull by the demise of the *Mellcrawler*.

Leia, eyes still dazzled, was trying to make sense of the battle around them. Flashes of light surrounded the *Shieldmaiden*, which was listing badly. She could see the triangular bulk of the other Star Destroyer—and the TIE fighters pouring out of its belly.

"How long until we can make the jump?" she asked Nien, wondering why the Sullustan seemed so calm.

"Thirty seconds," Nien said with a grin. "Scan shows the *Shieldmaiden*'s reactor is failing. We should wave good-bye."

"First we need to tell those other rebel ships to get clear," Leia said. "Kidi, can you raise any of them?"

"Yes—yes, I can," Kidi said quietly. "Now that they know we're safe, they're jumping."

"Good," Leia said. "But where did they come from? Whose task force is that?"

"You might say it's ours," Kidi said, and tears began to run down her cheeks. "They're the ships from the rendezvous—the ones you warned to flee. They came back."

"They did?" Leia looked at Kidi, astonished. "How many?"

"All of them."

CHAPTER 23
HONORING THE LOST

WITH THE SHUTTLE safely in hyperspace, Leia left the cockpit to check on Kidi, who had gone back to sit in the crew compartment.

"Are you all right?" Leia asked, taking her hand.

Kidi shook her head. "I can't believe he's gone. We'd barely gotten to know each other and now he's gone."

"I know," Leia said. "But you can't let your grief stop you from living. I've learned that. We have to live for those we've lost so that their memories are kept alive through us. Particularly those who sacrificed their lives so we could go on."

"Lok," Kidi said. "And Antrot."

"And the people we never knew," Leia said. "The crews of the ships that came to our aid, and the villagers in Jowloon, and the pirates on Sesid. We have to honor them by carrying on their fight."

"By doing our duty, you mean."

"That's part of it," Leia said, remembering Mon Mothma's words to her, before they'd set out for Corva sector.

"That's part of it, but now I realize there's something more important than that," she said. "We fight for a cause, but what we're really fighting for is each other. That's why our pilots fly into fire instead of abandoning a wingman and our commandos stand their ground rather than leave a flank unguarded. It's because they care for each other. We fight for duty, yes. But we also fight because we love each other. And that's something even more powerful."

"And do you think Lok loved me?"

"You don't need to ask me that," Leia said. "You already know the answer."

To Leia's amazement, Kidi managed to broadcast an encrypted transmission to R2-D2, and an hour later Leia was looking at a hologram of Luke.

"Mon Mothma's been beside herself," he said, smiling. "And I've been a little worried, too."

"I'm fine. Where are you?"

"Kothlis," Luke said, then peered at the hologram he was seeing of her. "Are you wearing an Imperial uniform?"

"I am," Leia said. "Its previous owner won't miss

it—she's space dust. Along with her Star Destroyer. Of which the shuttle *Tydirium* is all that remains."

"You'll have to tell me all about it when you get here. The fleet's nearly assembled. Plus we have new intel about Han. He's still in carbonite, in Jabba's palace. And I have a plan to get him out."

Leia looked down at her uniform. "I don't know your plan, but I've been thinking about a role I could play. I'll tell you about it when we reach Kothlis. And then we'll get Han and bring him back to us. Where he belongs."

EPILOGUE

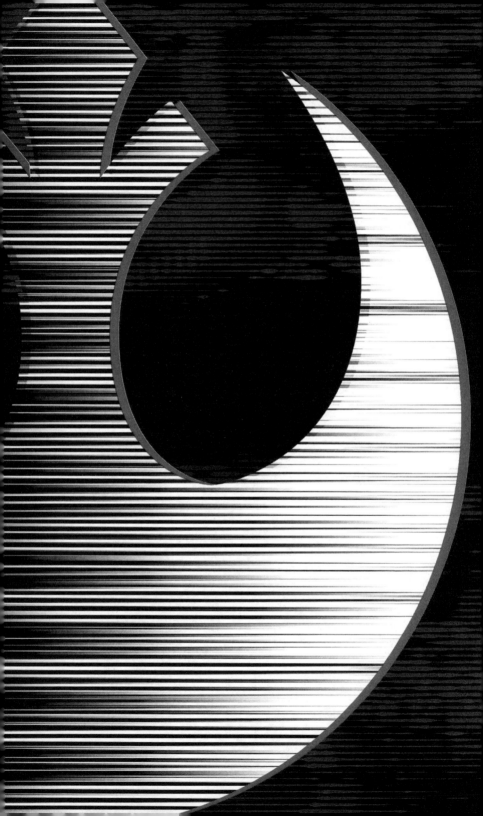

PZ-4CO SAID nothing for a long moment after Leia had finished, and she briefly feared that the protocol droid had shut down without her noticing. But then the droid's eyes brightened and the holorecorder sticking out of her chest turned off, then retracted into her torso.

Leia turned at the sound of her quarters' door chime.

"This is an excellent beginning, General Organa," the droid said. "Now perhaps we could discuss your childhood on Alderaan—"

"Some other time, Peazy," Leia said. "That's more than enough for one day. Besides, I have a visitor."

Ematt stood on the other side of the door.

"Major, how fitting," she said as the droid clanked away down the corridor. "I was just discussing the mission to Yellow Moon, right before Endor. You may recall you and Nien Nunb brought me to Zastiga, where it all started."

"Indeed I do," Ematt said with a nod. "What brought that to mind, if I might ask? Ah—you've finally agreed to dictate your memoirs."

"To start on them, at least," Leia said. "It was a question about duty—our commitments to causes, and to each other, and how we balance the two. It's something I learned battling the Empire, and now Poe's learning the same lesson against the First Order. I've discussed it with him. He's old enough to hear me, but not old enough to listen yet. I'll keep trying."

"Dameron's commitment is absolute," Ematt said. "And he's our best pilot. He'll get what we need."

"I've never worried about Poe's commitment. My worry is for what that commitment may cost him."

Ematt nodded, and Leia peered at him.

"I know that look," she said. "Is there news from Jakku?"

"Yes, General," Ematt said. "We're awaiting you in the command center."

Leia nodded and stepped into the corridor. The door shut behind her. As she and Ematt walked toward the command center, she felt a familiar tingle somewhere in the back of her mind. Events were in motion, and she would be at the center of them—at the center of the action.

And that, even after so many years of war, was a relief.

and she would be at the center of them—at the center of the action.

And that, even after so many years of war, was a relief.